A Mermaid in Middle Grade

in

Middle Grade

BOOK 3
VOICES OF HARMONY

KNOWLEDGE FOREST
PRESS

A.M. LUZZADER

Published by Knowledge Forest Press
P.O. Box 6331
Logan, UT 84341

Ebook ISBN-13: 978-1-949078-19-0
Paperback ISBN-13: 978-1-949078-17-6
Hardback ISBN-13: 978-1-949078-18-3

Cover design by Sleepy Fox Studio

Developmental and Copy Editing by Chadd VanZanten

Proofreading by Sandra Hutchinson

Interior illustrations by Chadd VanZanten

In memory of Simon

ACTIVITY KIT

Visit www.subscribepage.com/amandaluzzader to download a **Free Activity Kit for A Mermaid in Middle Grade.** You'll also be able to join my newsletter, but can unsubscribe at any time.

CHAPTER ONE

*M*ermaid Brynn Finley swam into her bedroom and went directly under her bed. If you knew Brynn, you'd be able to tell she was extra excited and enthusiastic on this particular Friday afternoon. When she emerged from beneath the bed, she held a large box. It was just an ordinary hat box, but if you knew Brynn, you'd know this was no *ordinary* hat box. It was decorated with pretty shells and bits of colorful coral and a pretty green bow. Brynn's eyes were bright and happy as she opened the box.

Inside was her extensive and impressive collection of Mermies.

Mermies were poseable dolls that young mermaids (and even some merboys) all over the sea loved to play with. Brynn's collection included Mermies of many varieties. Their hair was fixed in different styles and hues. They had various complexions and eye colors. There were mer-kids and mer-babies and handsome Mermie mermen. Brynn began carefully removing the Mermie dolls from the box.

There weren't just dolls in the box, of course. Inside the box were smaller boxes, compartments, and pouches, each filled to the brim with the Mermie accessories that Brynn had accumulated. In addition to the dozens of Mermie outfits, dresses, coats, hats, and hair-pretties, Brynn had toys for the mer-kids and ties for the mermen. Brynn's Mermies had miniature books, dishes, furniture, and even a little pink shellphone. One of the Mermies was a doctor and had a lab coat and a medical kit. Another was an undersea architect, with blueprints and drawing desk. The Mermies had a sports car and a big shell-a-vision and even a cute little pet dolphin.

"These Mermies have nicer stuff than most real merfolk," mumbled Brynn.

Brynn was setting aside and arranging the Mermies she planned to play with that evening. First there was the one with purple hair and a teal tail, whom Brynn called Rain. Next was her favorite merman Mermie, a doll she called Ben. When Brynn played with Mermies, she'd frequently conduct marriage ceremonies between Ben and Rain.

Then there was the beautiful Mermie with white hair, whom Brynn called Shine, and which Brynn felt more than just a little resembled her best friend in the entire world, Jade. If Brynn were being completely honest, she would admit that Shine was her most favorite of all her Mermies because the doll did look like a grown-up version of Jade.

If you knew Brynn, you'd know that the reason she was setting out her Mermies this way was because Jade was arriving soon for a sleepover. It'd been only a month since Jade's mother had accused Brynn of stealing her necklace and forbade the two mermaids from seeing each other. While that had led Brynn to forming a new friendship with a smart merboy named Will and some other merstudents, she had missed Jade terribly. They had a lot of catching up to do, along with playing Mermies and drinking kelpshakes and calling each other "dahling!"

Brynn was so glad that all the terrible trouble with Jade and her mom was in the past now. It had been discovered that the sea witch, Phaedra, and her assistant, Ian Fletcher, were responsible for stealing the necklace. The mer-police had apprehended them, and Brynn's name had been cleared at last.

Jade's mother, Mrs. Sands, felt awful for keeping the mermaids apart, so it wasn't surprising when she agreed to let Jade sleep over at Brynn's house. Both Brynn and Jade had been looking forward to this particular Friday for days and days.

Brynn brushed Shine's and Rain's hair, and then positioned them more carefully on her bed. They had to be just so.

Tully, her pet sea turtle, swam over and sniffed at the dolls.

"Don't mess those up, Tully," Brynn chastised. "Jade will be here soon, and I want everything to be perfect. We're going to have the bestest best-friend sleepover that there ever was! We'll play Mermies and listen to Jay Barracuda and the Killer Whales, and mom said we could have anchovy pizza and—"

Before Brynn could finish telling Tully everything she had planned for their sleepover, there was a knock at the door.

"Finally! It's Jade!" cried Brynn, and in the next instant, Tully was alone with the mob of Mermies and the trail of frantic bubbles Brynn left behind when she zoomed out of the room to answer the front door.

"Hi, Jade!" she cried as she yanked the door open.

But to her surprise, Jade wasn't the only mermaid there. Along with Jade was another young mermaid.

This other mermaid had soft, pink-colored hair into which was pinned sparkling sea glass and shells. Also, her ears were pierced—something Brynn's mother had said Brynn wasn't old enough to do. Brynn was certain she'd never seen this mermaid before, but she also had to admit that the newcomer was very beautiful. The mermaid's long and slender tail glinted in metallic shades of green, violet, and blue.

"Brynn," said Jade, "meet Priscilla Banks. Her

family just moved to Fulgent. I invited her to join us for the sleepover."

"Oh, hi, Priscilla. It's nice to meet you," said Brynn, and she tried to say it like she meant it, and under different circumstances, she probably would have. In fact, there was something familiar about Priscilla. Had they met before? It didn't matter. But Brynn had spent the entire week planning and waiting and looking forward to her Mermies sleepover with Jade—*just* Jade.

"It's nice to meet you, too," said Priscilla.

Was there something strained in Priscilla's voice?

"So," said Jade, "will it be all right if Priscilla joins us tonight?"

"Uhm, well, I guess," stammered Brynn, her mind racing. Did she know Priscilla already? But more importantly, what kind of mermaid just barged into a sleepover like this? "We'll, uhm, we'll have to check with my mom, I suppose," Brynn stammered, still trying to sound more pleased than she felt. Priscilla seemed nice, but why'd she have to show up *now*? Why tonight? Why with Jade? Why couldn't the sleepover go as planned, with just Jade and the Mermies and the music and the anchovy pizza and—

"Uhh, hey, Brynn?" said Jade.

Brynn blinked back to the present moment. "Huh?" she grunted.

Jade chuckled and said, "Are you—ya know— gonna invite us in?"

"Oh! Sure! Of course. Come on in!" Brynn laughed nervously. "Sorry. Where are my manners? Ha ha. Gee. Yes, come in."

Jade and Priscilla were both holding overnight bags and pillows. They swam into the living room and set down their things. Priscilla looked around the living room of Brynn's house with one skeptical raised eyebrow.

Brynn noticed and asked Priscilla, "Is something wrong?"

"No, no," said Priscilla. "It's just, your house is so—"

"So—what?" said Brynn, folding her arms.

"So—cozy," said Priscilla.

"You mean *small*?" asked Brynn, placing her hands on her hips.

"Well, yes, but that's not so bad, is it?" said Priscilla. "Small can be good. I bet your housekeeper can finish up fast!"

"Housekeeper?" Brynn was feeling more than a little annoyed. Who was this mermaid?

Jade jumped in. "Hey, Brynn, maybe we should find your mom and make sure it's okay if Priscilla stays the night."

Brynn shot Priscilla a sideways glance and said, "Yeah, maybe you're right, Jade. Hey, mom!"

"Yes, dear?" Her mother was in her room on the other side of the cave, but in just a few seconds, she appeared in the living room.

Brynn had never thought of her family's home as being small. It always seemed like the perfect size. Besides, their coral cave was similar to many of the mer-homes in Fulgent. Brynn looked around, trying to imagine what it'd be like to see her home for the first time.

"Brynn?" her mother said.

Brynn blinked again back to the present. "Mom," she said, "Jade's here for the sleepover, but she has this friend with her." She turned to Priscilla and said, "I'm sorry—what was your name again?"

Jade elbowed Brynn and scoffed. "Brynn," she whispered hoarsely, "her name's *Priscilla*."

"Right," said Brynn. "Priscilla, a mermaid I don't know and have never met before, is here and wants to sleep over, too, but I know that's probably a bad idea because she just moved here, so it's not okay, right?"

"Nonsense!" cried Brynn's mom with a grin. "Priscilla is perfectly welcome to stay the night! Priscilla, I assume you've checked with your parents?"

Priscilla nodded and shot a knowing glance at Brynn.

"Then there's no problem," said Brynn's mom.

"Great," Brynn muttered. "What a relief."

Jade jumped in again. "Fin-tastic! Let's get our stuff and get this party started!" As the young mermaids picked up their overnight bags, Jade leaned over and whispered to Brynn: *"What's the matter with you?"*

"Where did you move from, Priscilla?" asked Brynn's mom.

"I used to live in Atlantis," Priscilla said with a sigh. "It was *the* most beautiful place. But then my father decided we needed to move here. We hired a pod of whales to move our entire chateau to Fulgent."

"Brynn, you have to see her home!" Jade squealed. "It's huge! And it's all made of white stone; it's so pretty."

"Sounds—really—swell," said Brynn.

Priscilla shrugged. "It's all right," she said.

"Hey," said Brynn. "Are you wearing makeup?"

It was more of a statement than a question, because it was quite obvious that Priscilla was wearing makeup, and not just a little lip gloss and blush like Brynn's mother sometimes let her wear, but glittery bright eyeshadow and mascara and—was that highlighter? Brynn thought Priscilla looked just like one of the models in *Young Mermaid* magazine.

"Of course I'm wearing makeup," said Priscilla. "Do you like it?"

"Sure," said Brynn, she was thinking that Priscilla seemed a lot older than she and Jade. "So you go to the high school, then?"

"I wish," said Priscilla, who was examining her manicured fingernails.

"She's in sixth grade, silly," Jade answered. "Same as us."

"What? Did you get held back or something?" asked Brynn.

"Brynn!" Jade chastised.

Brynn shrugged frantically at Jade.

"No," responded Priscilla, sounding bored. "I'm twelve. Like you. You just think I look older because you don't know about make-up and fashion out here in this backwater burg. Back in Atlantis, all the sixth-grade mermaids wear makeup, and you can't tell us apart from the high-school mermaids."

Brynn hadn't really thought much about wearing makeup other than for dance recitals or real dress-up occasions. And so she felt a little nervous around Priscilla, and she wasn't sure if it was because she was in awe, or intimidated, or just jealous.

But she wasn't going to let this change of circumstances ruin the fun evening she had planned.

"Well, anyway, let's go to my room. I've got everything ready," said Brynn.

The three mermaids swam to Brynn's room.

"Whoa," said Priscilla as they entered Brynn's room. "How are all three of us supposed to fit in *here*? Is there a guest bedroom somewhere? And it's so dark—how do you see in here?"

As with the rest of her house, Brynn had never thought about the size of her room before, or about it being dark. This had always been her bedroom, and it had seemed perfectly fine up until that moment. Priscilla's comment about the size and lighting of Brynn's bedroom made her cheeks feel hot. Half of her wanted to defend her home and the other half just wanted to hide.

While Brynn contemplated the state of her bedroom and how to respond, Priscilla spotted the Mermies that Brynn had lovingly arranged on her bed.

"Oh, cool, Mermies!" said Priscilla with a funny laugh.

Brynn smiled. Maybe Priscilla wasn't so bad after all. It could be fun to have a new friend to come over and play with Mermies.

"I used to play with Mermies all the time!" Priscilla picked up Shine, the doll with the white hair. "So, you've got a little sister? And you both live in this little bedroom?"

"I don't have a little sister," said Brynn.

"Oh. Then these are your little brother's?" said Priscilla, holding up the doll and shrugging one shoulder.

"I don't have any brothers or sisters," said Brynn. "These are mine. All of 'em."

Priscilla's tail fin waved through the water, and she smirked. "They're yours? Wow. I thought only *little* mermaids played with Mermies. No one in sixth grade at my old school played with Mermies."

Brynn huffed and asked, "What do they do for fun?"

Priscilla shrugged. "Go to the mall, hang out, talk on the phone, whatever. But we certainly don't play with little dolls."

Brynn was speechless, and if you know Brynn, that didn't happen very often. She shot a glance at Jade, which Jade correctly interpreted as, "What in the sea is going on here?"

Jade erupted with a hasty, nervous laugh. "Um, yeah, Brynn. Mermies were cool when we were little mer-kiddies, but we don't play with them anymore, do we?"

Brynn's mouth dropped open and she blinked many times in rapid succession. "What are you talking about, Jade? We played Mermies all day just a week ago. Priscilla is holding Shine, your favorite Mermie!"

"Oh, Brynn, Brynn, Brynn," said Jade with more nervous laughter. "You—are—such—a—kidder!"

Brynn held up her hands. "Hold on, Jade," she said. "You're saying you *don't* like Mermies?"

"Not—any—more!" said Jade, and she scowled at Brynn, which Brynn correctly interpreted as "Just go along with what I'm saying because you're embarrassing me in front of Priscilla!"

Brynn huffed but decided to play along. Jade was her best friend, after all. Brynn forced a loud laugh and said, "Right, right. We used to play with these dumb dolls all the time, but not anymore, of course."

"Then why are they all laid out?" asked Priscilla.

"Hmm?" puzzled Brynn. "Oh! Yes. Well, I was going to throw them out, see, since I haven't played with them in so long."

"Yeah," answered Jade. "Might free up some room in here."

Brynn harrumphed.

"You know," continued Priscilla with a smug smile, "if you're in the middle of cleaning out your room, we could always move this sleepover to my place. It's much larger and brighter, and it'd probably be a lot more fun."

"Maybe another time," said Brynn. "My mom's getting us anchovy pizza, and I've got a movie for us to watch."

"What movie?" Priscilla asked.

"'While You Were Swimming'," answered Brynn.

"Oh, I've already seen that," said Priscilla. "Very boring. Not worth watching. But if you come to *my* house, we can play with the new Orpheus Shell my dad bought."

"Oh, wow!" said Jade. "You have an Orpheus Shell? I've only seen those on shell-a-vision."

"They're super fun," said Priscilla.

"What's an Orpheus Shell?" Brynn asked.

"It's a pod made from a giant shell. You sit inside and it plays music and has a light display and gives you a massage and there's aromatherapy. It's very posh," said Priscilla. "Only two people can be in it at once, but we can take turns."

"That sounds fin-tastic!" said Jade. "It must have cost a million sand dollars."

Priscilla shrugged again.

"Well, I don't think my mom will want me to sleep over there. She was already planning on us doing stuff here," said Brynn.

"Let's ask her," said Jade, and before Brynn could respond, Jade was already swimming down the hallway.

"Wait!" yelled Brynn. But by the time Brynn and Priscilla followed after Jade, she had already found Brynn's mom, Dana, in the kitchen.

"Brynn wants to know if she and I can sleep over at Priscilla's house," Jade said.

Brynn glared and grumbled. This sleepover was not going as she'd planned.

"Well," said Dana thoughtfully. "I'm all in favor of making new friends, but I haven't met Priscilla's parents yet, and it seems a little late in the day to be making such big plan changes."

Brynn smiled. For once, her parents' silly rules were working *for* her, instead of against.

"Let's just stick with the plan for tonight, girls," said Dana.

"Guess we'll just have to stay here," said Brynn with fake disappointment.

Priscilla raised an eyebrow and said, "Jade, *you* could still sleep-over at my house."

"Whoa, whoa, whoa," Brynn objected. "Hold your seahorses there. Jade is here to have a sleepover with *me*. We've been planning this all week!" Brynn felt her heart pounding, and her tail felt shaky. She'd met this Priscilla only minutes before, and suddenly everything was floating sideways. She glared at Priscilla who has examining her nails again without an apparent care in the world.

"Mrs. Finley, could Brynn at least do a late-over?" asked Jade. "She could just hang out with us at Priscilla's house until it was time for bed and then you could pick her up?"

Dana Finley considered this with a tilt of her head. "I suppose that would work. Okay then, you mermaids have fun! I'll pick up Brynn this evening. What's your address?"

"Mrs. Finley, have you seen the white and gold castle not far from the elementary school?" Jade said.

"Oooh," said Dana. What was it that Brynn heard in her mother's voice? Surprise? Or was she impressed?

"Sure, I know where that is," said Dana. "I couldn't miss it."

"That's what everyone says," said Priscilla.

Brynn was so surprised at this weird turn of events, she didn't know quite what to say. She was glad to be able to hang out with Jade, but she was so angry at Priscilla for barging in and changing all the plans, but she also knew that Jade liked Priscilla, so she wanted to be nice to Priscilla, too, but she felt something else. Could it be jealousy? Brynn shook her head. Why should she feel jealous? Brynn and Jade had been best friends since they were mer-babies. Just because Priscilla was beautiful and rich and new that didn't mean it would change anything between her and Jade.

Or would it?

CHAPTER TWO

*J*ade wasn't joking when she said that Priscilla's house was huge. "House" wasn't the right word. "Mansion" was closer, but still didn't properly capture the building's proportions and towering size. This was an estate, a kingdom, Brynn thought, and the "house"?

"No, fortress," Brynn thought. Priscilla lived in a fortress.

The three mermaids entered the grounds, but still had a far way to swim before reaching a huge wrought-iron double gate at the base of the hill upon which the home sat. They could have swum over the gate, but it seemed more polite to wait as the gate swung open on its own, as if someone were expecting them. There was probably a spell on the gates, Brynn figured.

They swam on. Brynn and Jade gaped and stared

at the statuary situated around the grounds, the groomed kelp and seaweed, and reefs of coral grown into the shapes of dolphins and whales and giant squids.

They approached the palatial facade of the immense home. There stood soaring marble columns and tall windows. The double doors of the main entrance must have been as tall as three grown mermen.

"How have I never seen this place before?" Brynn asked.

"Because it wasn't here until recently," said Priscilla. "Like I said, Mother and Father hired a whole team of whales—blue whales, of course—to move it over in pieces from our old estate in Atlantis," said Priscilla. "Then we had a large crab-struction crew and merfolk working to assemble it. It only took a week."

Brynn couldn't even imagine how many merpeople and crabs must have been working on it to have gotten it assembled so quickly. Maybe hundreds.

The front doors swung inward and the mermaids swam into a large rotunda—a circular gallery with a high, domed ceiling. If anything, this was even more stunning than the outside of the building.

"Wowee," said Brynn softly.

She almost felt as though she should swim face-up, to see all the marvelous architecture. It was like something from a movie or a dream. The marble walls and columns were inlaid with darker stone and accented with bright coral. The columns were topped with vivid green sea moss that waved in a gentle current.

It became clear now why Priscilla thought Brynn's house was rather small. Brynn was certain three of her houses could fit inside just this large round entryway—with room to spare.

Light filtered down from many windows along the dome and set into the walls, which made it feel almost like they were still outside. Along the margins of the round space, there were statues—mythical and legendary sea creatures cast in bronze and marble. The floor was splendidly tiled with brilliant mother-of-pearl.

And at the center of the rotunda, there stood a fountain that produced a dazzling flume of bubbles and streams of air. The bubbles burbled up to the ceiling, where they escaped from special openings in the roof. There were large bubbles and bubbles so tiny they seemed like mist. And bubbles in large, surprising bursts, and bubbles in thin, delicate lines and spirals.

Neither Brynn nor Jade had ever seen anything like Priscilla's house. Brynn's mouth hung open in amazement. Jade likewise stared in astonishment at the soaring, elegant interior. Priscilla only looked bored.

As Brynn and Jade marveled at the intricate patterns the bubble-fountain produced, they spotted something drifting down from an upper level. It was a merman, floating downward and through the bubbles. He moved with a certain self-confident dignity, his hands clasped behind him and his tail waving slowly, but powerfully. His hair was purple and combed back from his forehead. His tail shimmered in dark reds, greens, and blues.

"Well, hello there!" he cried when he saw the mermaids. He smiled broadly at them. "Priscilla! Back so soon? And you've brought friends! Splendid! Splendid!"

"Yes, Father," said Priscilla. "This is *my* friend Jade, and *her* friend Brynn."

Brynn wasn't at all pleased with that introduction, but what could she say?

"Welcome, mermaids! Welcome!"

"Thanks, Mr. Banks," said Jade. "Your home is fin-tastic!"

Priscilla's dad fussily adjusted an expensive-looking vase made of bright gold china and decorated in coral-colored sea flowers, which stood on a pedestal nearby. Then he turned to Jade and said, "I'm glad you like it, my dear. Is anyone hungry?"

"I think we're all hungry, Father," said Priscilla.

"Splendid," said Mr. Banks, rubbing his hands together. He seemed genuinely pleased. "Well, then. Why don't you three dash off and play at whatever it is mermaids of your age play at, and I'll tell Seasworth to whip up some anchovy pizza and big bowls of fish cream. When you're ready, just ring the bell. How's that sound?

"Thanks, Father," said Priscilla, still sounding slightly bored. "Come on," she said to Brynn and Jade. "Let's go to my room and try out the Orpheus Shell."

"It's in your room?" Jade exclaimed. "Can I be your new best friend?"

Brynn winced. Jade was just joking, right? Either way, it stung. Jade was so impressed with Priscilla and her house and everything about her. Brynn could hardly blame her, of course—everything about Priscilla seemed amazing. So why was Brynn constantly glaring at Priscilla whenever her back was turned?

"I don't think I'd like living here," said Brynn quietly to Jade as they followed Priscilla to her room.

"Huh? Brynn, are you kidding? Look at this place. It's so huge, I don't know if we're inside or outside!"

"That's what I mean," said Brynn, keeping her voice low. "It's so huge and lonely. And the decorations are a bit much, don't you think? It'd be like living in a museum."

"Yeah, a museum with a bubble fountain and maids and a butler who makes you pizza anytime you want—oh! and an Orpheus Shell *in your room! This place is fin-freaking-tastic!*"

Brynn frowned, though she tried not to let Jade see. Did this mean she'd have to try extra hard to stay friends with Jade? Would they still be besties?

They all swam into a room, and, sure enough it was bigger than the entire sea cave where Brynn and the rest of her family lived. Everything was decorated in white and gold and looked very refined and elegant. And tidy—Priscilla's family must have had an entire staff of maids and house cleaners. No mer-kid kept their bedroom this neat. There was a huge four-poster princess bed in the center of the room (perfectly made), beautiful draperies on the windows, a shell-a-vision, and lots of pillows and plush chairs to relax in.

"Welcome to *my* room," said Priscilla, gesturing at the enormous space.

"Woooah," said Jade. "Now this is a bedroom! What do your parents do for a living?" Jade asked, obviously wondering how Priscilla's family could afford such luxuries.

"They invented these," said Priscilla. She held out her long, elegant arm. Around her wrist was a sparkling bracelet inset with a watch. "We moved here so they can oversee manufacturing."

"No way!" cried Jade, her eyes wide. "Your family invented Swymbits?"

"What's a Swymbit?" asked Brynn.

"It's a watch," said Priscilla.

"Oh," said Brynn. "Well, I guess it's pretty."

21

"Priscilla! Tell Brynn it's not just an ordinary watch!" Jade gushed. "It's so much more! It can play music and videos, it can track how far you swim in a day, it can record your fitness and heart-rate, and it measures your magical energy. You can play games on it. There's so much you can do with it."

Jade grabbed Priscilla's arm and stared at the Swymbit. "Fin-tastic!"

"They're pretty expensive, I guess," said Priscilla. "But I could probably get you two some discounts so that you could afford them. Father has a goal to get everyone in Fulgent to wear Swymbits."

Brynn scrunched up her face. "No thanks. I don't think I'd like it."

"Could you really get me a discount?" asked Jade, practically giggling with glee. "I'll ask my mom."

"No biggie. Look on the Interwet later and tell me which one you want," said Priscilla. "But for now, let's use the Orpheus Shell. Which one of you wants to go in with me first?"

Jade instantly shot her hand into the air. "Me, pick me!"

"Okay," Priscilla said. "You can use it with me first and then, Brynn, you can have a turn."

From under her gigantic bed, Priscilla pulled out what looked like a huge closed clamshell with a pearly finish. It was only a little smaller than the bed. Priscilla pushed a button and the shell opened revealing two reclining seats with plush pink fabric.

There were speakers and a screen and a miniature refrigerator. Even Brynn, who was trying very hard to not be impressed by anything in Priscilla's house was absolutely blown away. It looked like so much fun.

"The seats actually form to your body," said Priscilla. "And then it gives you a head-to-tail massage. You can pick a cold drink from the dispenser. There's over one hundred flavors."

Jade quickly dived inside the shell. "I can't wait! Let's try this!"

Priscilla joined Jade in the other spot, and then turned to Brynn. "It takes like fifteen minutes, but then you and Jade can switch. I get two turns because it's mine." And then she pressed a button and the shell closed, and the two mermaids disappeared inside.

The shell must have some kind of sound insulation because Brynn couldn't hear Jade or Priscilla at all. In fact the room was very quiet, and she felt very alone. She began looking around the room. It really was beautiful.

What did Priscilla do to deserve such a nice room? Brynn wondered, and suddenly, she was feeling a little angry. The more she thought about Priscilla the angrier she got. It wasn't just that Priscilla's family was rich, it was that Jade, Brynn's best friend since forever, was so impressed by it all.

Brynn thought back to her sea cave home and her

tiny bedroom and her old Mermies. Jade had been okay with all of that before, but how could Brynn compete with all of this? What did Brynn have that was as interesting or fun as an Orpheus Shell?

As she waited for the two mermaids to emerge from the Orpheus Shell, Brynn envisioned Jade becoming more and more interested in Priscilla and less interested in her.

She imagined Jade saying, "I'm sorry I can't hang out with you Brynn. Me and Priscilla have plans. Just the two of us. She really is the best thing that ever happened to me." Then off she'd swim with a flip of her tail, leaving Brynn behind in a cloud of lonely bubbles.

Brynn tried to shake the image from her mind, but all she could picture was Priscilla and Jade laughing as they swam away, best friends, and Brynn alone with her Mermies.

This was worse than when Jade's mother wouldn't let Brynn play with Jade. At least then she knew Jade still *wanted* to be her friend. What could be done when someone you liked so much didn't want to be your friend anymore? Brynn swam around Priscilla's room looking at her expensive belongings, trying to find something to distract her.

She floated over to a dresser and noticed a picture frame sitting in front of a large mirror.

Inside the picture frame was a front cover of *Young Mermaid* magazine—the same magazine that she and Jade both had subscriptions to. They had spent many hours side-by-side looking over the pages of the magazine, reading every word of every issue. Brynn recognized the cover, of course; it was from last year. There was a fun quiz in the issue about what job you'd have when you grew up, and an article about the latest in sunglasses for wearing on the surface. But why would Priscilla have the cover of an old magazine in a picture frame?

Brynn picked it up from the dresser to look at it more closely. Then her mouth dropped open.

Just then, the Orpheus Shell opened and Jade and Priscilla tumbled out laughing.

That's why Priscilla seemed familiar! Priscilla's face was on the *cover!* Her hair was fashionably styled, and she was peering over the top of a pair of very chic sunglasses. Brynn turned to Priscilla and Jade, still holding the framed magazine cover.

"Y-y-you're a model for *Young Mermaid?*"

Priscilla swam closer and looked at the framed cover. "Oh, yeah," said Priscilla. "That one was memorable. It was one of my first covers."

Jade rushed over to look as well. "Oh, wow!" she cried. "I cannot believe this. I have that magazine! You're, like, famous, Priscilla!"

Priscilla shrugged. "I guess."

"Come on," said Jade. "Admit it! You're famous! You are the most famous person to ever live in Fulgent! And I get to be your friend! I am *so* lucky!"

It was all too much for Brynn. She'd been jealous before, but nothing like this. Priscilla had her on the verge of tears—and all she did was *exist*. Priscilla had everything anyone could ever want, and now Brynn found out she was a cover model for her favorite magazine.

But that wasn't the worst of it—Priscilla was stealing Brynn's best friend right out from under her nose.

"You *have* to teach me how to do makeup," squealed Jade. "Teach me how to be a model."

Neither Brynn nor Jade had worn much makeup before—at least not besides the play makeup they had used with their moms. Brynn did want to wear makeup—someday—but she didn't think her parents would want her wearing too much quite yet.

"Sure, we can put on some makeup," said Priscilla with a shrug. "But first, we need to let Brynn have her turn in the Orpheus Shell."

Brynn set the picture frame back on the dresser. She felt hot tears forming in her eyes.

"I don't feel very well," mumbled Brynn. "I better go home."

"Really?" Priscilla asked. "We still have a few hours until your mom was going to pick you up. You sure you want to leave? Seasworth will have that pizza ready soon, and the fish cream. And you didn't even get your turn yet, though if you think you might puke, I'd rather you not use it."

Brynn nodded.

"Oh, Brynn," said Jade. "I'm sorry you don't feel well."

"I just want to go home," said Brynn. She gathered up her things, and Priscilla went to tell her mom that Brynn wasn't going to stay.

Brynn thought she'd just swim home alone, but Seasworth objected.

"Tut tut, miss. I'd be derelict in my duties if I let someone your age swim home unaccompanied. You'll take the sea-copter."

Mr. Banks agreed, and in a flash, Brynn was swept to the landing pad. Seasworth the butler stood with Brynn as the sleek, shining craft swooped in and made its landing. The sea-copter resembled a large squid, but it was made of glass and metal, with eye-like windows in the front and propellers at the rear.

"Good evening, Miss Finley," said Seasworth warmly. He made a slight bow to her. "I do hope you feel better soon and visit us again. Our sea-copter pilot's name is Rick. He'll see you safely home."

A door opened and Rick, the pilot, greeted Brynn politely. Then he motioned her into the cabin. There were plush seats inside and portholes to see out. Rick worked the sea-copter's controls and the engines hummed to life. Soon they were cruising smoothly through the sea on the way to Brynn's house. Under different circumstances, Brynn would have thought this sea-copter ride was the coolest thing ever. After all, she didn't even know very many merfolk who'd been given a personal ride on a sea-copter.

But Brynn was more glum than she had been in a long while, and the sea-copter ride was just one more reminder of all the excitement Priscilla experienced every day, so she couldn't properly enjoy it. The smooth, luxurious ride of the beautiful and sleek watercraft only made Brynn feel worse.

CHAPTER THREE

*D*ana Finley, Brynn's mom, was just getting ready to make herself a cup of seaweed tea when she heard strange noises coming from outside. It was whirring and whooshing. She looked out the kitchen window but saw nothing out of the ordinary, so she went to the living room and looked out of the front window. There in the front yard sat a luxury sea-copter. It was shiny and streamlined and beautiful. Dana thought briefly how she'd wanted to ride in a sea-copter ever since she was a little mermaid, but the opportunity had simply never come along.

She opened the front door, as if she didn't fully believe what she was seeing through the window. However, sure enough, the sea-copter was there, humming softly, on the Finley's front yard. As Dana's eyes widened, a port opened on the near side of the sea-copter, and Brynn swam out.

"Brynn?" cried Dana.

When Brynn was a few tail-wags from the sea-copter, the shimmering machine's propellers whirred smoothly and the sea-copter lifted off, climbing into the water above the little sea cave homes of Fulgent. Soon it disappeared in the evening ocean gloom.

"Yes, Mom," said Brynn glumly.

"You—you got a ride home in a sea-copter?"

"Yeah," said Brynn, passing by Dana and swimming into the living room.

"Hmm. You don't seem very excited. How was it?"

"Oh, it was just *swell*."

Dana could tell something had gone wrong for Brynn that evening, but she didn't think it was a good idea to pry just then. Instead she asked Brynn, "So, Priscilla's family has their own sea-copter?"

"Of course they do," moaned Brynn, throwing her arms in the air. "Doesn't every little mermaid have a private sea-copter and a butler and a bedroom big enough to park a blue whale in it?"

"I've always wanted to ride in a sea-copter," said Dana wistfully. "They have a butler, too? Wowee."

Brynn sighed and swam off to her room. It pained her to realize that it wasn't a very long swim. She closed her bedroom door behind her, but Dana soon knocked. Brynn opened the door.

"So, why'd you come home so early?" Dana asked as she floated into Brynn's room. "I thought you were going to stay until bedtime."

"I wanted to come home," said Brynn. "I told Jade and Priscilla I wasn't feeling well."

"Oh no," said Dana. She pressed her hand on Brynn's forehead. "Hmm. You feel clammy," said Dana. (Merfolk are supposed to feel clammy, of course, so this didn't concern Dana.) "Are you sick?"

"Well, not exactly. I was just sick of the way Jade and Priscilla were acting."

"Ah." Dana nodded sympathetically. "They were being mean?"

Brynn thought about this. "Yes," she said.

"What were they doing?"

"Jade was completely ignoring me. She only talked to Priscilla, and she was acting like we weren't even friends. Priscilla is a big snob, and she just likes to show off everything because her family is rich or whatever and they own the Swymbits company." Brynn collapsed onto her bed. Talking about it was making her feel even angrier. It just wasn't fair!

Dana sat on the bed but was quiet for a while. "Is it possible that you're feeling jealous?" Dana finally asked.

"I'm not jealous!" Brynn said. "They're the ones who are being mean. Jade especially. She's *my* best friend, but she sure didn't act like it."

"It's good to make new friends," said Dana. "It

sounds like that's what Jade is doing. Couldn't you be friends with Priscilla, too?"

"I don't want to be friends with her. The only reason Jade likes her is because Priscilla's family is rich, and she's got a lot of nice stuff."

"That sounds really sad to me," said Dana.

"What do you mean?" Brynn asked.

"I dunno," said Dana. "I think most merpeople want people to like them for who they are, not what they own. Don't you think Priscilla probably feels that way, too?"

"What difference does it make?" Brynn asked. "She has *everything*."

"Well, I know some things she doesn't have," said Dana.

"No, mom, she literally has everything. That sea-copter was theirs. She has an Orpheus Shell. She even has a modeling contract with *Young Mermaid*!"

"Well, Priscilla doesn't have Brynn Finley's imagination or sense of humor. And she doesn't have Dana or Adrian Finley for parents. And she doesn't have a sweet turtle named Tully."

"Mom, I gotta tell ya—she didn't seem too disappointed about any of that."

"Brynn, I know it's difficult when you see people who have more than you. Especially when there doesn't seem to be any reason why they deserve it. But you'll drive yourself crazy trying to compare what you have to what others have. The best thing to do is to find the happiness in your own life. Every merperson has good things in their life and hard things."

"Not Priscilla Banks," said Brynn. "She only has good things."

"*Every* merperson," said Dana. "Just because you might not see it, that doesn't mean Priscilla has a perfect life. There are things that are hard for her, too. For example, I bet it was hard for her to move from Atlantis to a new area where she doesn't know anyone. And maybe she had a best friend that she left behind."

Brynn thought about how it would be if she had to move far away from Fulgent and couldn't be friends with Jade anymore.

"Maybe she's even scared that she won't make new friends," said Dana.

"Well, she doesn't have to steal mine!" Brynn said.

"That's right," Dana said. "Jade can be friends with both of you. And you know what else? You can be friends with both Jade and Priscilla. Maybe try it. You never know."

Brynn folded her arms and sulked. The last thing she wanted was to be friends with Priscilla Banks. What she really wanted was for Priscilla Banks to go back to Atlantis!

CHAPTER FOUR

On Monday, Brynn got up early. She swam past her pet sea turtle, ate clamcakes for breakfast, and got ready for school with loads of time to spare. She had spent practically the whole weekend sulking, moping, and sighing sadly. She watched the shell-a-vision without really paying much attention, and generally did not have fun. Her attitude hadn't improved much as she approached the speed-current, but in the back of her mind, she was quietly hoping that the whole dreadful business with Priscilla and her stupid castle-house and her dumb Orpheus Shell and her butler and her stealing Jade would simply blow over and be forgotten. Brynn hoped that things between her and Jade would start over somehow, or reset, like a shellphone.

But that was not to be.

Brynn came closer to the speed-current stop and saw Jade, who smiled and waved. However, as Brynn came closer, her heart sank when she noticed a sparkly new accessory on Jade's wrist.

"You got a Swymbit?" Brynn moaned.

"Yeah!" Jade bubbled. "Come and check it out! It's really cool!" Jade said, holding up her wrist and fiddling with the tiny buttons. "I wanted one just like Priscilla's, but hers is way expensive. I had to settle for this one, but it's still pretty awesome."

Brynn didn't like seeing Jade wearing the Swymbit. It was just another sign that Priscilla was winning the friendship contest, and that Jade was picking Priscilla over Brynn.

"Do you really like it?" Brynn asked. "It seems kind of clunky and pointless. Won't your arm get tired?"

"Are you kidding? It's fin-tastic! I love it!" said Jade. "Look! I've got three fitness goals, and I've got all my music downloaded, and I can set an alarm to wake me up, and there's games and—"

Brynn sighed heavily as Jade prattled on about the sparkly gizmo. "So, what did you guys do after I left?" Brynn asked when Jade paused to take a breath.

"Oh, you know, we just hung out. It was really fun. I'm sorry you were sick. Are you feeling better today? Speaking of which, after school Priscilla and I are going to Mammoth Cave to practice singing.

35

Omigosh, Brynn, you should hear her sing. She's got a beautiful voice. Come with us and listen. It's amazing."

Brynn rolled her eyes so hard she thought they might pop out and float away. Was there anything about Priscilla Banks that wasn't absolutely perfect? She could sing, she was a model, she was cool, and now she was winning over Brynn's best friend.

Like all mermaids, Brynn could sing, but it wasn't her favorite thing to do. Her voice was pretty enough, and she could use her singing to amplify and improve her spell-casting, but no one at Crystal Water Middle School would ever accuse her of having the best voice of all. Dancing was Brynn's thing. That's how it'd always been—Brynn was the dancer and Jade was the singer. But Priscilla's talent gave her yet another advantage in the friendship battle, and there was no way Brynn was going to just swim away from this and let Priscilla win.

"Oh, I'll definitely be there," said Brynn with a bit of snark in her tone. "Especially now that I don't have to worry about the sea witch."

She was referring, of course, to Phaedra the sea witch. Phaedra hated humans and the way they polluted the oceans, and on two separate occasions, Brynn had interfered with attempts by Phaedra to sink human ships. Phaedra was not only stunningly beautiful, but she had incredibly powerful magical abilities. She could control the weather, and it was rumored that she could turn mermaids into sea slugs.

Phaedra had sworn to get revenge on Brynn, but luckily, the mer-police had captured Phaedra, and they were presumably doing all they could to prevent Phaedra from casting spells and keeping her detained.

"Did you see on the news that Phaedra's going to trial soon?" Jade asked. "I saw it on the shell-a-vision at Priscilla's house."

"Yeah, it's about time," said Brynn.

Her parents had explained to her that even though Phaedra had been captured in the act of sinking ships and causing other problems, there still had to be a trial, where evidence was presented and everyone would get to tell their side of the story, even Phaedra. Then a jury, a group of seafolk from Fulgent and the surrounding area, would decide if Phaedra was innocent or guilty. If the sea witch was found guilty, a judge would decide if there should be punishment and what it might be.

Because Phaedra's crimes were serious, and because she'd been guilty in the past, it was expected that she would go to jail again, but the court system still had to do things officially and go through the process to make sure it was fair.

"They said on the Night Sea News that the trial should be wrapping up this week," said Jade.

"Good," said Brynn. "I'll feel a lot better once I

know that she won't be able to get out for a long time."

The two mermaids got on the speed-current.

"So, you'll come to Mammoth Cave with us to practice singing?" Jade asked.

"Are you sure you don't want to do something else? Singing's okay, but isn't there something else you'd like to do?" Brynn asked. "We could go to the kelp forest and play hide and seek, or maybe there's something *else* you'd like to play?"

Brynn was thinking of her Mermies, obviously. She felt so bad when Jade said she didn't like playing with them anymore, and she wanted to know why. Had she really given up playing with Mermies, or did it have something to do with Priscilla? However, Brynn didn't want to bring it up. Brynn was still very into Mermies, but Priscilla's teasing had made her feel embarrassed about it. Along with everything else she was good at—singing, modeling, acting cool— Priscilla was also apparently good at making people feel embarrassed. But even if Priscilla and Jade thought they were too old for it, Brynn didn't agree. In fact, Brynn thought she might always enjoy playing with her Mermies. Was there anything wrong with that?

"Brynn, you know I like singing," said Jade. "I'd love to be in a band someday. If you don't want to come, that's fine, but we're still going to go."

Brynn wanted to insist, even demand that Jade do

what Brynn wanted instead. It made Brynn frustrated. How could she get Jade to see things her way? Brynn decided that she'd just have to go along with them and show Jade that Priscilla wasn't such a super awesome mermaid after all.

It was a weird day at school for Brynn. She wanted classes to be over so that she could go to Mammoth Cave with Jade and Priscilla. She wanted to go because it was her chance to get a head in the friendship battle. On the other hand, Brynn was nervous about the whole thing—few things impressed Jade like good music. If Priscilla was as good at singing as Jade said, that might be the deciding factor in the friendship battle.

Brynn's hesitation and anticipation combined to make the day pass very slowly, but then when the final bell rang, she couldn't believe the school day was already over. She had a full-blown case of the jelly-fish-jitters as she gathered up her school supplies and prepared to meet Jade and Priscilla.

When Brynn got to the speed-current stop, Jade and Priscilla were fiddling with their Swymbits.

"Hi!" said Brynn.

Jade looked up and cried, "Hi, Brynn!"

But Priscilla barely looked up from her Swymbit. She quietly said, "Hi," but that was all.

They got on the speed-current route to Mammoth Cave, but it felt a lot like a repeat of the demolished sleepover—Jade and Priscilla talked excitedly with each other, leaving Brynn practically by herself. To Brynn, the ride seemed to take forever.

Mammoth Cave was out near the Craggy Deep, and it wasn't like the caves that most merpeople live in. For one thing, it was huge, with walls of smooth, curved rock. Also, merpeople came from all over to use it as a performance space. There was a large, flat stone that served as a stage, and there was an area where a large audience could gather to watch and listen. Behind the stage there were hollows and alcoves that could be used to store stage scenery and change costumes.

As the mermaids swam into the vast cavernous place, Priscilla sang a few notes.

And her voice was lovely. Her pitch was perfect and the sound seemed to shimmer like sunlight on gentle ocean waves. And this was just a warm-up! She trilled and la-la-la'ed and sang a few scales. The lovely notes echoed off the cave walls and then moved through the water like a cool, gentle current. Even Brynn was impressed and wanted to hear more.

I'm doomed, thought Brynn, *absolutely doomed!*

"I like the acoustics in here!" said Priscilla. "Thanks for bringing me here, Jade. I love it. This will be a great place to practice some songs."

"I just thought after your first day of school, you might like doing something fun," said Jade. "How was your first day, anyway?"

Priscilla shrugged. "It was all right. There were so

many people, and I didn't know any of them. To be honest, it was a bit tiring and overwhelming trying to get to know so many new people."

"Oh, poor Priscilla," mocked Brynn. "I bet it's really hard making friends when you're a model and you're rich and talented and you never have to clean your enormous *bedroom*."

Brynn knew it was wrong to say such things. She had been absolutely terrified on her first day of middle school. She got befuddled and lost and the day was actually quite disastrous. But Brynn wasn't thinking of that at the moment. She was thinking desperately of anything she might say to prevent Jade from getting to be better friends with Priscilla.

"Brynn!" Jade chastised.

"Actually, it is difficult," admitted Priscilla. "Before this, I'd lived in Atlantis my whole life, and I didn't really want to leave. I still don't." For a moment it seemed as though Priscilla might cry. "I wake up every morning thinking I'm still there, then I realize I'm not."

"Pff!" scoffed Brynn. "You live in a castle, Priscilla! No, not even a castle! A palace! Ten palaces stacked on top of each other! Are you really complaining?"

"Brynn," said Jade softly, "you aren't being very nice."

"Neither are you!" Brynn insisted, pointing a finger at Jade. "You two have been ignoring me.

What happened to me being your best friend, Jade? What about that?"

"We're *still* best friends!" cried Jade. "What is *with* you lately?"

Brynn could see that they were about to have a big blowout fight, but to her surprise, Priscilla stopped it by suddenly singing a popular song.

"Come swim in the ocean. Come swim in the sea. There's beauty around you. Now don't you agree?"

Wowee, thought Brynn. *Priscilla really is a great singer. A really, really great singer.*

Brynn knew Priscilla could have easily ganged up on her with Jade, but instead she just sang a little bit of a pretty song. Hearing her voice made Brynn and Jade instantly stop fighting just to listen to her.

But somehow, Brynn still wasn't happy. In fact, she wished that Priscilla had been a lousy singer. And part of her felt happy that Priscilla had a difficult day. She hoped things would get even more difficult for her, and then maybe the whole rich Banks family would move back to Atlantis.

Brynn couldn't say or even figure out in her own mind why she felt this way. The simple truth was she was incredibly jealous, and she felt threatened by Priscilla. But all those rotten feelings were hiding behind Brynn's fear that Jade would stop being her friend. And even after all that had happened just a month ago with Jade and Will, Brynn had forgotten how it was possible (and even very fun) to have more than one friend.

Meanwhile, Priscilla kept on singing. Her voice radiated through Mammoth cave like sunlight, rich and warm and comforting.

"We are mermaids! Beautiful mermaids! We'll weather any storm, save each other from the swarms. Best friends we'll always be, the prettiest fishes in the sea."

Brynn was sitting on a rock a little distance away from the other two mermaids. Jade waved her tail to the beat of the tune Priscilla sang. After a while, she joined in and sang along. Singing together, Priscilla and Jade's voices harmonized perfectly, creating not only spectacular and harmonious chords, but also a gold glowing light that flowed from their voices. This was a well-known mer-magical effect of beautiful harmony—mer-magic seemed to simply materialize from the sea all around them.

Jade and Priscilla smiled at each other and nodded as they went on singing.

Brynn, on the other hand, lowered her eyebrows and puffed out her bottom lip, like a wee mer-baby who wants a toy she can't have. Brynn had decided that she was *not* going to let this be some fancy-shmancy mer-magical moment between Jade and Priscilla that would bond them together forever.

And she knew what she had to do to break the spell.

With an angry grin on her face, Brynn took a deep

breath and then joined in the singing herself, belting out each word as loudly as she could. She was a little off-key and she jumbled up some of the lyrics, but there was no doubt that Jade and Priscilla heard her. Brynn's voice reverberated off the cave walls like a sea elephant colliding with a tugboat. Even after the magical glow winked out, and even after Priscilla and Jade made sour faces and covered their ears, Brynn went on blaring out the song until she wasn't singing at all but only shouting a series of disconnected notes and sounds.

"Brynn, what are you doing?" Jade asked.

"Singing," said Brynn. "Same as you."

"Well, okay, but do you have to do it so—so loudly?" Jade asked.

Brynn shrugged.

Priscilla was staring at her Swymbit. She tapped it, and then she tapped it again.

"What's wrong?" Jade asked.

"My Swymbit. It stopped working." She kept tapping at it. "It's like it just turned off for no reason. And I know the battery was more than halfway charged."

Jade looked at the Swymbit on her own wrist. "Mine stopped, too," she said.

"I know that mine was working a minute ago," said Priscilla. "I looked at it right before we started singing."

Priscilla and Jade both looked at Brynn.

"Oh, come on," Brynn groaned. "I don't sing *that* bad."

"I dunno, Brynn," said Jade. "I've heard you sing before you were all the way warmed up before, but this time you were *trying* to sound bad."

"No," said Priscilla, who was now trying to reset or reactivate her Swymbit. "I don't think singing would interfere with a Swymbit. I's probably just a coincidence."

"Two Swymbits turning off for no reason almost at the exact same time?" said Brynn, raising one eyebrow. "That's an awfully big coincidence, don'tcha think? Sounds to me like they're maybe not made very well."

Priscilla's face flushed, but she didn't answer. "Could be a bug in the latest update," she said. "That would explain why they both turned off at the same time."

"Well, what should we do?" said Jade.

"My father can probably fix them both, but we should go to my house right now so that he has time to work on them before dinner."

"Really, we're leaving now?" Brynn asked. "We just got here."

Jade looked up from her Swymbit. "Brynn," she snapped, "*you* don't have to come with us, because *you* don't have a Swymbit."

"She's right about that," said Priscilla. "Now you can stay here and 'sing' all you like."

45

Brynn huffed.

"Don't worry, Jade," said Priscilla. "My father has a little workshop and everything. I'm positive he can fix it."

"Gosh," complained Jade. She looked like she was trying to tap the screen and push every button on the gizmo at the same time. "It really just won't turn on! This is terrible. I just got it. And it wasn't cheap, you know."

"Well, let's go," said Brynn and she started swimming toward the speed current.

"Why do you want to come?" asked Priscilla. "Like Jade said, you don't have a Swymbit, and you obviously don't care that ours aren't working. We're not going to hang out and put on lipstick. We want our Swymbits to work. I have fitness goals to work on and make-up videos to watch!"

"You guys don't want me to come?" Brynn asked.

"It's not that," said Jade. "You'll probably just be really bored. We all know you don't like the Swymbits."

Brynn blushed.

"Okay, well, I'm sorry your Swymbits broke," mumbled Brynn.

Priscilla and Jade shrugged, and the three mermaids gloomily swam off to catch the speed-current. It was growing dark now, and they spoke little during the ride. At the stop where Jade and Brynn normally would exit and swim home together,

Brynn rose and hopped off by herself. Then she watched as the current carried away her best friend.

On the ride home, Brynn had been thinking. At first, she didn't think her intentionally bad singing had caused the Swymbits to malfunction, but even though it sounded odd, Brynn wondered now if she really had somehow caused the incident.

What is it about Priscilla that makes me act like that? Brynn wondered as she swam home through the gathering darkness.

As Brynn neared her home, she saw a dark shape coming her way. The evening was coming on fast, and she squinted to see what it was.

"Tully!" said Brynn.

The little turtle must have been at outside and detected Brynn, and he had come out to greet her. He swam a few circles around Brynn and then swam a few more circles in the opposite direction. Her licked her face and wagged his stubby little turtle tale.

The two were only a short distance from home. The appearance of her pal Tully had made her feel a bit happier, and this got her thinking a little clearer. She recalled the time when she and Jade had welcomed Will, a merboy, into their friendship, even though he had sometimes said rude things. There hadn't been any issue once they'd both gotten to know Will, and the merboy had helped Brynn with important problems on several occasions. Now both Jade and Brynn were quite fond of Will, and he was fond of both of them. In fact, Brynn and Jade's friend-ship with each other seemed to somehow improve after Will came along.

So, why was it so different with Priscilla?

Tully glided on ahead of Brynn, sniffing and snuf-fling at the coral and chasing jellyfish. Brynn had to admit that her biggest worry was not that Jade would be friends with Priscilla, but that Priscilla would replace Brynn in Jade's life. A busy young mermaid only had so much time and energy. There were classes to pass, magic spells to cast, and most mermaids in middle-school were going on sea guardian rescue missions nowadays. If Jade spent all of her free time with Priscilla, she wouldn't be able to spend time with Brynn. It was a simple matter of mathematics.

I'm being silly, Brynn thought. *Jade would gladly make time to hang out with me.*

But what about the math?

CHAPTER FIVE

The next morning, Brynn got up, took Tully for a swim, ate her clamcakes for breakfast, and then got ready to depart for the speed-current stop to go to school. Again she hoped that the Priscilla problems of the previous day would simply be forgotten and that she could press the "reset" button on her friendship with Jade. As she headed for the door, however, she heard her mom's shell-phone ringing.

Dana answered the phone and then called to Brynn. "It's for you, Brynn" she said. "It's Jade."

Brynn had a quizzical look on her face as she took the phone from her mom, and before she even put the phone to her ear, Brynn could hear mermaids giggling on the other end.

"Hello?" Brynn said.

"Hi, Brynn," said Jade. "I just wanted to tell you

to not wait for me at the speed-current stop. I ended up sleeping over at Priscilla's house last night, and so her dad is going to take us to school."

"You slept over at Priscilla's house?" asked Brynn. "On a school night?"

"I know," giggled Jade, her voice distorting through the shell-phone speaker. "Weird, right?" But we were over here getting our Swymbits fixed, and then we had a snack, and then it got late and we were having so much fun, my mom made an exception and said that I could."

Having so much fun? Making an exception on a school night? They're pushing me out! Brynn thought.

Brynn clenched her jaw. "Well, did you get your Swymbits fixed?" asked Brynn, hoping beyond hope that they were broken forever.

"Oh, sure," Jade answered. "Priscilla's dad said the microphones must have been blown out when you sang so loud in the echo-chamber of Mammoth Cave. But he got them both fixed and everything is great now."

Even though they were speaking over the shell-phone, Brynn blushed. "I wasn't *that* loud."

"Yeah, Mr. Banks said it probably had something to do with the acoustics or something. Don't feel bad. We both know you didn't do it on purpose. But, hey —maybe try not to do it again, okay?"

"Sure, um, okay," said Brynn.

"All right, well, they've made a huge breakfast for

us—clamcakes stacked a mile high, so I better go. I'll see you at school! Goodbye!"

Brynn was about to ask Jade if she wanted to go to the kelp forest or listen to Jay Barracuda records or something after school, but before she'd said anything, Brynn heard more gales of giggling and fun through the shellphone, and then the line went dead.

Brynn handed the phone to Dana and frowned.

"What's the matter, Brynn?" asked Dana. "What did Jade want? Is anything wrong?"

Not just anything, Brynn thought, her face growing hot. *Everything is wrong.*

"Brynn?"

Brynn wanted to answer, but couldn't think of how she could easily explain it all before she had to leave for the speed-current stop. So, she simply said, "No, everything's *fine*."

But the way she growled the word "fine" left no doubt about how she felt, and Dana watched Brynn mope out of the front door. Brynn swam to the speed-current stop and waited for five minutes to get on the speed-current before she remembered that Jade wasn't coming. It had just become so natural to Brynn to wait at the stop for Jade, or for Jade to be there first. This gave Brynn a little sad pain. She got on the speed-current, found a seat well away from the other riders, and sat gloomily for the ride to school.

She was still lost in her thoughts, trying to figure out why all of this made her so upset, and trying to make a plan of what to do about it, when Will, her other best friend, swam up and sat next to her. Will was a very good friend and had helped Brynn a lot over the past year. He was smart, kind, and good at magic.

"Hey, Brynn," said Will. "How's it going?"

She almost blurted out the whole story to Will. Brynn knew he'd understand, and he'd probably have some good ideas about what to do next, but the whole stupid situation was just so upsetting, all Brynn could manage to do was grumble the word *"fine"* again.

"Oh," said Will. "That bad, huh?"

Brynn rolled her eyes.

"Say," Will continued. "Where's Jade?"

"Her mom let her have a sleepover with the new girl, Priscilla, so *they're* taking her to school today."

"A sleep-over? On a school night?"

"Yeah."

"Wow," said Will. "That's cool."

"No, William Beach, it's *not* cool. Lately, Jade has been completely obsessed with Priscilla, who has a butler and parents who invented the coolest sea-lectronic device in the whole ocean, and a bedroom bigger than my whole house, and they're probably on a sea-copter right now eating fresh oysters and candied kelp and homemade fish cream with three housemaids to clean up after them."

Will didn't understand everything Brynn said, but he understood enough. "Feelin' left out, eh?"

"Left out?" whined Brynn. "They've practically left me in exile! They invite me to Priscilla's castle and then don't talk to me. They invite me to Mammoth Cave and then ignore me. And now here I am on the speed-current all by myself, and you know what? She's not even that great! Have you even met her?"

"Priscilla Banks? Yeah, I met her yesterday. I thought she was really nice. She helped me get on the Interwet and get one of these for a killer sale price."

Will held up his wrist to reveal a new Swymbit, with a hip striped band.

Brynn moaned. "Aaah, not you too? Why does everyone love her so much?"

Will shrugged. "I don't know. She's nice and interesting. Why does she bother you?"

Brynn fumed. Her mind raced with nasty, unfriendly thoughts. Why *did* Priscilla bother her? *Because I'm nice and interesting, too!* she thought. *But nobody is paying attention to me!*

"I just don't think she's as great as everyone else thinks she is," Brynn finally huffed.

"You know, Brynn," said Will in his snarky way, "just because someone else is getting compliments or attention, that doesn't say anything about you, you know? Besides, remember how you told me that it was good to have more than one kind of friend, even more than one best friend? Why don't you just be friends with her, too?"

"Because you're assuming two things, William Beach. First, you're assuming that *I* want to be friends with Priscilla, which I do *not*! You are also assuming that Priscilla wants to be *my* friend, which she obviously doesn't, or she wouldn't be constantly trying to steal the friends I've already made!"

"What other friends besides Jade is Priscilla supposedly stealing?" Will asked.

"Well, she hasn't even been here a week and now both of my best friends have Swymbits! What's next? Pretty soon you'll all be cozied up in her Orpheus Shell without me!"

"I thought the Orpheus Shell only had room for two people at a time," said Will thoughtfully. "I guess we'd have to take turns."

"Will!" shouted Brynn, causing other speed-current riders to turn and look. In a quieter voice, she continued. "That's *not* the point. The point is, pretty soon the whole school will be her best friend and I'll be left all by myself!"

"How come you don't want to be friends with her?" asked Will.

"It's not that," said Brynn. "We're just so different. She and Jade are so into singing and makeup and stuff and I"—Brynn didn't finish her sentence, but what she wanted to say was, *"and I still want to play Mermies with Jade."*

Brynn stared out of the speed-current watching the ocean landscape change as the current sped them along toward school.

After a while, Will asked, "Are you worried that Jade just isn't going to like you anymore?"

"Yes! That's exactly it," said Brynn.

"Ah, Brynn, I don't think you need to worry about that," said Will. "You two have been best friends forever. Everyone in school knows you two are the best best-friends in the whole universe of best friends."

But Brynn *did* worry about it. She'd been worrying about it for days. And she would continue to worry about it. In fact, when at last the speed-current dropped them off at Crystal Water Middle School, and Brynn began noticing just now many kids were now wearing Swymbits, she got very worried indeed.

When Brynn got into the lunch line—still without Jade—she overheard two mermaids talking. "I wanted one just like Priscilla's. And look, mine is almost just like hers!"

And it wasn't just in the cafeteria. *Every*where Brynn went that day, she heard mer-students chattering excitedly about Priscilla. The entire school was acting like Priscilla was some kind of celebrity.

"Did you know she is a fashion magazine

model?" "She lives in a castle!" "Have you seen her private sea-copter?" "Priscilla sings better than anyone I've ever met." "If she went on The Ocean's Got Talent, she'd win for sure!"

After that last comment, Brynn rolled her eyes and swam away. She was positively sick of hearing about Priscilla Banks. She had only two things to look forward to that day. She couldn't wait to go home and lock herself into her room so she wouldn't have to see, hear, or interact with Priscilla Banks. However, before that, Brynn was looking forward to her Beginning Magic class, taught by Windy Meyers. Brynn liked many of her school classes, and there were some that she didn't like very much. But something about Beginning Magic class always made Brynn feel great. It was something about the way Ms. Meyers explained things and was so kind and understanding. The class was always a highlight of Brynn's day, even if she was having problems. Today Brynn was definitely having a problem, and the problem's name was Priscilla.

"I'll feel much better after Ms. Meyers' class," said Brynn to herself.

When it was finally time, Brynn took her regular seat in Ms. Meyers' classroom and breathed a contented sigh. Will came in and sat behind Brynn, like he always did.

"How ya' feeling?" Will asked. "How are things going?"

Brynn turned around in her seat and answered, "Things are going just great—!"

Will answered, "Oh, that's good."

"—if you're in the Priscilla Banks fan club!" she finished, her voice icy.

Will shook his head. Brynn often wished she could be like Will—nothing ever seemed to bother him.

"I don't know why you don't like her," Will said, looking down at his Swymbit and tapping on it. "She's really cool."

Brynn turned back around and crumpled down into her seat. Nothing ever seemed to upset Will, but sometimes he just couldn't understand how she was feeling. She slumped down even farther.

However, just then, Ms. Meyers swam into the classroom. Now Brynn sat up straight in her chair, and she smiled. Whenever Ms. Meyers came into a room, it was like the sun coming up, or a warm current of summer ocean water, and Brynn really did start to feel better almost immediately.

Brynn wanted to be just like Ms. Meyers when she grew up. She admired just about everything about Ms. Meyers. You could say Ms. Meyers was Brynn's hero. She was smart, successful, beautiful, terrific at mer-magic, stylish, funny, friendly, great with students, and—

—and Mrs. Meyers wore a brand-new Swymbit on her wrist.

Brynn's mouth dropped open and she felt almost as though she would cry. "I don't believe this," growled Brynn, turning around in her seat to face Will. "Does *everybody* have one?"

"Hmm? What?" asked Will, looking up. "Sorry, what'd you say? I was reading this article on my Swymbit about the National Fishbowling League."

"Aw, forget it," muttered Brynn, and she slumped in her chair again.

CHAPTER SIX

*D*espite Mrs. Meyers' surrender to the Swymbit zombies, Brynn really did feel in slightly better spirits after class was over. Something about the way Mrs. Meyers explained things that day cleared Brynn's mind and settled her emotions. And when the class was over, Brynn had a plan. This wasn't a complicated plan, like her plans often were. And it wasn't a plan that could go all sideways and get Brynn into lots of trouble that she might not have anticipated. No, this plan was very simple, safe, and smart.

Brynn decided that all she really needed to do was to spend some quality time with her best friend, the friend she'd had since they were wee mer-babies, the friend who'd never ever let Brynn down: Jade.

That'll fix everything, thought Brynn. *I guess it's not*

*so horrible if Jade has another friend who lives in a palace,
as long as she and I can still be besties.*

Brynn hadn't seen Jade much at school that day,
and she didn't see Jade after school. Brynn had been
a little late getting to the speed-current stop, and so
she thought that Jade must have gotten on and
headed for home without Brynn. So, instead of going
straight home, Brynn rode the speed-current to Jade's
house.

Mrs. Sands, Jade's mom, answered the door.

"Hello, Brynn!" said Jade's mom. "It's nice to see
you! I don't think I've seen you at all for a week!"

This remark hit Brynn like a rock on the head, but
she knew Mrs. Sands didn't know about the Priscilla
problem, so she ignored it.

"Hi, Mrs. Sands!" said Brynn with a big smile.
"It's good to see you, too. I've missed coming over.
Anyhow, is Jade here? Can she hang out today?"

Mrs. Sands face clouded. Maybe she did know
what was going on. "Oh, I'm sorry, Brynn," she said.
"Jade's already been here and gone again. She was
headed over to Priscilla's house. But she left only a
little while ago. Maybe you can catch her, and the
three of you can hang out together."

To her credit, Brynn really was trying hard to be
more like Will at that moment. Jade had gone to
Priscilla's house without even inviting Brynn, but
Brynn tried not to let anything bother her. Instead,
she said, "Okay. Thanks, Mrs. Sands!" and she swam

off in the direction of Priscilla's house (or palace, fortress, or mansion—whatever it was).

Sure, Brynn would have preferred just spending time with Jade alone, but hanging out with Priscilla too would be better than not seeing Jade at all. So, she put on a brave face and did not change her plan.

When Brynn got to Priscilla's house and had swam across the vast grounds of the estate and through the big iron gate and then onward to the immense double doors, Seasworth answered.

"Why, it's Miss Finley," said the butler warmly. "Delighted to see you again, my dear. May I presume you are looking for Miss Banks and-or Miss Sands?"

"Yes, Seasworth," said Brynn, and she had to admit it was nice to have such a pleasant mer-fellow around to help you with things. "Are they here?"

"I'm very sorry, Miss Finely. I'm afraid your mermaids friends have been here and now have gone. But I heard them squealing something about going to Mammoth Cave to practice singing, so I'm sure you'll find them there. It's not very far from here, of course, but shall I call the sea-copter pilot to take you there? It shan't be a moment—"

"No, no!" said Brynn. "That, uhm, that shall not be necessary, Seasworth. I shall, um, proceed there by my, um, self."

"Very well," said Seasworth with his trademark bow. "If you're sure?"

"Yes, yes," answered Brynn, "that shall be all."

Brynn's shoulders slumped as she swam away. *They didn't even ask if I wanted to come,* she thought glumly, and at first, she intended to go to the cave and demand an explanation for why they hadn't invited her. Then, however, Brynn realized if she did that, she'd just end up crying. Besides, she didn't want to risk breaking their Swymbits again. So, instead, Brynn sadly swam home.

When she got there, her dad had the shell-a-vision on and Tully was sitting on his lap. The pet turtle perked up when Brynn entered, and he swam his usual circles around Brynn by way of greeting.

Well, if I can't spend time with Jade, this is probably the next best thing, Brynn thought giving Tully a pat on the shell. *Dad will be watching something so super boring that my brain will go numb, and Tully's around to keep me company.*

Brynn took a spot on the couch and Tully settled in between Brynn and her dad. Brynn gave the turtle a good head and neck scratching. Tully cooed with delight. On the shell-a-vision there was indeed some kind of boring news coverage playing. There were mer-police officers and merfolk in business suits, and Brynn thought she saw a merman in some kind of black robes, like a judge.

"What's this?" Brynn asked, not really caring much, hoping only for something so dull it would cross her eyes.

"Funny you should ask," said Adrian. "It's a live

broadcast of the trial of your old friend the sea witch, Phaedra. Looks like she's finally having to face the consequences for her choices."

Brynn stared at the screen, suddenly interested. Seafolk of all kinds milled about the scene. There were merpeople, selkies, and dagons. There were lawyers and reporters and police and court workers. In front of the courtroom sitting at a high desk was the judge, the Honorable Matthew Waterly, a merman with short, silvery hair and spectacles on his small nose. A reporter said that Judge Waterly had a reputation for being one of the fairest judges around.

"Wowee," breathed Brynn, settling into the couch cushions. "This looks intense." She watched for a few minutes, waiting for something to happen, but as it turned out, it really was quite boring. The sea witch wasn't even in the courtroom yet. Various reporters and experts were discussing the case, but not really saying much, and there was a lot of legal mumbo-jumbo that even her dad didn't seem to comprehend.

Brynn scratched her head. "Is she going to get away with it?" she asked.

Adrian shook his head. "Not a chance. They have a mountain of evidence against her. It's going to take several days just to hear all the testimony from the witnesses, but then she'll go to jail for sure."

"Oh," said Brynn.

She was glad that the sea witch wouldn't be around to turn her into a slug, but even that news didn't cheer her up much. The news reporters droned on, predicting what would happen and what would not happen. Brynn's father grabbed the remote and snapped the shell-a-vision off.

"Eh. Enough of that," said Adrian. "I think you and Tully and I just having a chat would be more interesting."

Brynn shrugged.

"Something bothering you?" Adrian asked. "You haven't seemed yourself lately."

Brynn shrugged again. "Yeah," she said. "There's this new girl at school. Priscilla. And Jade's been spending so much time with her."

"And you're feeling a bit left out?" Adrian asked.

Brynn nodded.

"And maybe you're feeling that you're not as special or interesting as this new girl?"

Brynn nodded again.

"I see," said Adrian. "That must be really hard. No one wants to feel left out."

"I just want Jade to realize that I'm still cool, too. She used to think I was awesome until Priscilla came around," said Brynn. "Now I'm nobody. I don't have a butler or sea-copter or Orpheus Shell. I don't even have a lousy old Swymbit."

"You're still awesome, though. You know that, right?" said Adrian. "You have a good heart, Brynn, and you're brave and smart and a lot of other wonderful things. There's only one Brynn Finley, and she can't be replaced."

Brynn shrugged. She didn't feel that great. "I guess," she said.

"You know what I think?" asked her dad. "I think we should plan something really fun for just us to do. It can be a father-daughter date. Whatever you like."

Brynn's dad could be a really fun guy, but if Brynn were being honest, she didn't want to hang out with him. What she really wanted to do was just slouch on the couch and watch Judge Matthew Waterly mutter about proceedings and listen to news reporters trade theories about the sea witch. Then Brynn could just sort of doze off into a bored daze and hope things would go better tomorrow. She didn't really feel like hanging out with her dad, but she didn't want to hurt his feelings, so she shrugged and said, "Sure, Dad. I guess that sounds fun."

"What would you want to do?"

"I don't know."

"Come on, get creative. I'm giving you a blank check here. If you could do anything, what would you want to do?"

Brynn gave it some thought, cheered up a little, and then sighed. "I guess we could get some clamburgers and kelpshakes."

"Brynn! Think big! Think fun! We can get clamburgers any old day. Let's do something we've never done before. Something that excites you."

Brynn couldn't think of anything. She couldn't think of a single thing that might excite her.

Adrian snapped his fingers. "How about this? Jay Barracuda and the Killer Whales? I did some catering for them, and they liked the food so much they said I could have some tickets to their next concert, which I believe is next weekend."

Brynn sat up. "I love JBATKW!"

"You love what now?" said her dad.

"Jay Barracuda and the Killer Whales!"

"Oh! Right JBATKW! Of course you love them!" cried Adrian. "Everybody knows that!"

Brynn hadn't thought there was anything that she could be happy about while she was having these friend troubles, but she suddenly felt super excited.

"Really?" she said. "We can go?"

Adrian nodded. "Think it will help cheer you up?"

"Oh, yeah!"

"Then Brynn and her dad are going to the JBATKW concert!"

"Thanks, dad," said Brynn. She gave him a big squeeze. Tully was apparently feeling a bit left out, too, just then. He shoved his way between them to share the hug.

Of course, the first thing Brynn wanted to do was call up Jade to tell her about the concert. The two best mer-friends told each other everything, no matter how trivial. Once, Brynn had called Jade just to describe a new hairbrush she'd bought with her allowance, and they ended up talking about it for two hours. Sometimes, Jade and Brynn would just get on the phone and say nothing while they did their homework or watched shell-a-vision. With big news like this, Jade and Brynn's friendship procedures would ordinarily require Brynn to immediately call Jade and tell her the news. In fact, Brynn was already reaching for the phone, as though her hand was going to follow the procedure with or without her. But then Brynn remembered that Jade and Priscilla were hanging out together. Without her.

And so she drew her hand back. Then, however, Brynn bit her lip, picked up the phone, and dialed.

"Will?" she squealed. "It's Brynn! You're *never* going to believe what concert my dad is taking me to next week!"

CHAPTER SEVEN

*J*ade wasn't waiting at the speed-current stop the next day, either, but this time she hadn't called, so Brynn rode to school by herself again. Brynn spotted Jade in the hallway when she got to Crystal Water Middle School.

She swam over to Jade and put her hands on her hips. "Jade, what happened this morning? I waited for you at the stop, but you never showed up."

"Oh, my oceans, Brynn! I totally forgot to tell you. I came to school earlier so that Priscilla and I could practice a song together. We're thinking of trying out for the school talent show."

"That's great," said Brynn with an obviously sarcastic tone. Brynn was also trying hard to keep from shouting or crying or shout-crying, and so she quickly swam past Jade and continued on to class.

"Are you angry?" Jade called after her.

Brynn turned to face Jade. "I don't want to talk about it right now. We can discuss it on the speed-current on the way home."

"Oh." Jade made an embarrassed face.

"What? You're not riding the speed-current home either? Another singing practice? Another sleepover?"

"Uh, yeah. Sorry. I'm going home with Priscilla," said Jade, her eyes downcast.

"Fine. Whatever. That's really great," said Brynn.

"Why are you so mad?" Jade asked.

"I just don't think it was really nice for you to leave me floating at the speed-current stop this morning. And it wasn't nice for you two to go to the cave yesterday without me."

"How'd you know we were there?" asked Jade, cocking one eyebrow. "Well, it doesn't matter. We didn't invite you because I know you don't like singing. And can you really blame us after last time? You broke our Swymbits."

Brynn's chin quivered. She wanted to tell Jade that it really hurt her feelings to be excluded. She wrapped her arms around herself. Brynn wanted to say that it felt like she was losing her best friend, that she was being ignored, that she was being shunned, even. However, Brynn knew that if she even tried to say any of this, she'd start crying.

Jade was smiling and waving to merkids passing

in the hall. Apparently, Jade didn't understand how upset Brynn was.

Brynn took a breath and managed to say, "I just don't feel like we're good friends anymore, not as close as we used to be."

Jade lowered her eyebrows and folded her arms. "Well, maybe we're not. I like hanging out with Priscilla, and she likes hanging out with me. There's nothing wrong with that."

"But, Jade, *we* used to be best friends."

"What do you mean, 'used to be'? It seems to me like *you're* the one who has decided not to be best friends anymore," said Jade.

Brynn just couldn't understand what was happening. It was like she was watching their friendship dissolve while all she wanted was to tell Jade that she was upset.

"I've got to go," said Brynn.

"Yeah. Well. Me, too," said Jade, and with a flip of her turquoise tail she turned and swam down the hallway.

At lunch, Brynn and Will sat together.

"You are going to love the Jay Barracuda concert! The music! The energy! The lights! The dancing!" said Will.

"Uh huh," said Brynn. She was barely listening to Will. She was too busy watching Jade and Priscilla, who were sitting across the lunchroom. The mermaids were chatting happily and showing each other their Swymbits and laughing. Occasionally, they even burst into songs.

"Brynn?" said Will, snapping his fingers in front of Brynn's face. "You with me? Tell me what you're planning to wear to the concert."

"Huh? Oh, I don't know. I have decided yet." Her eyes wandered back to Priscilla and Jade on the other side of the cafeteria.

"You should wear something with sparkles," suggested Will. "Maybe it will catch Jay Barracuda's eyes. He'll sometimes invite merkids up onto the stage to dance and sing. Can you imagine if that happened to you? I mean, I know the chances of that happening are small, but still—"

"Uh-huh," murmured Brynn.

"Oh, and after the performance you should try to get a set-list. That's a list showing the order of the songs that the band uses for the concert. They keep a few on the stage. Sometimes you can get a band member or a stage manager to give you one at the end. They're collector's items. Oh, and don't forget to get a t-shirt!"

"Mm-hm," Brynn answered without really answering.

"Brynn?" said Will. "What is with you?"

Brynn shook her head. "Huh? What?"

"I've been talking for like five minutes, and you've hardly heard a word I said."

"Oh, sorry," said Brynn, still looking at Jade and

Priscilla.

Will followed Brynn's gaze and realized what she'd been staring at all this time.

"Will you ever stop obsessing over them?" said Will.

"I was just thinking that maybe I should tell Jade that she has to pick. Either me or Priscilla."

"I think that'd be a bad idea," replied Will. "Wasn't it just a few weeks ago that you were telling me how great it is to have more than one friend?"

"This is different, Will. They're leaving me out. Pushing me out, really. I was Jade's friend first. That should count for something."

"Do you really think if you force Jade to pick one of you that she's going to pick you?"

Will's words stung, and now Brynn couldn't keep the tears from forming in her eyes.

"Thanks a lot, Will," Brynn said sarcastically as she hastily picked up her tray to clear it.

"Wait, that's not what I meant," said Will. "What I mean is that you can't force someone to pick between friends. It's a terrible idea. I feel really bad that you're being left out, but I'm still here for you, and you've got fun stuff in your life, too. You've got tickets to see Jay Barracuda and the Killer Whales! And next semester you'll be back in your dance lessons. Maybe you should just leave things alone for a bit and let Jade come back to you in her own time."

Brynn set her tray back on the lunch table. "But

what if she doesn't? What if this is the end of our friendship?"

Will sighed. "I don't know, Brynn. What if it is? You can't control others. And it is sad and unfair, and I totally understand how you feel, but Brynn, there's a million merkids who would love to be your friend. If Jade can't make time for you, then maybe find someone who will. You know you can always hang out with me."

Brynn said, "Thanks a lot, Will," and this time she meant it, but it wasn't the answer she wanted to hear. She wanted Will or her parents or someone to tell Jade to be a better friend to her. She wanted Jade to realize how hurt she felt. She wanted things to go back to the way they were before.

Somewhere deep inside of Brynn, everything Will said made sense. But Brynn just couldn't admit it. She was too hurt, too angry, and too afraid. The rest of the school day passed in a blur. On the ride home, without Jade again, Brynn felt absolutely numb and just wanted to crawl into her bed. She was hardly aware of what was developing around her, that is, until she got off the speed-current at her stop.

CHAPTER EIGHT

The undersea town of Fulgent was a beautiful little town. The tidy little sea-cave homes were surrounded with beautiful kelp and sea plants that waved serenely in the current. The coral reefs shone vividly in the sunlight and glowed softly at night. Schools of flashing fish roamed through the water above. Colorful crabs, sea stars, and octopuses crawled along the sea floor below.

But it was also a small town. Most everyone knew each other, and it was usually a quiet and peaceful community. And so even though Brynn had been in a bit of a daze for the whole day, when she got off the speed-current at her stop, even she could sense something was different. There were lots of excited conversations, and there was a weird energy in the air.

Then, on her way home, Brynn always passed by the Fulgent Courthouse. It was a large and stately structure made of coral and mighty sea stones near the middle of town. As Brynn came near the courthouse, she saw a crowd there—lots of merfolk, but others, too, like selkies and dagons, as she'd seen on the news report. Brynn knew they didn't live in Fulgent, and so she had wonder why they'd taken such an interest in the sea witch's case.

She swam closer to the courthouse, and saw that many of those gathered were angry and restless. Brynn was used to seeing people come and go from the courthouse, but most everyone in Fulgent knew each other and lots of them were good friends. Or at least friendly acquaintances. The people crowding around the courthouse that day, however, were definitely not waving and saying, "Hello! Nice day, isn't it?"

Instead, they seemed to be waiting impatiently for something to happen.

As Brynn continued on past the commotion and toward home, she thought she saw someone in the crowd scowl at her. It was a dagon, someone Brynn didn't know. Then, to Brynn's astonishment, this dagon tapped a selkie on the shoulder and pointed at Brynn. The two whispered to each other and pointed at her again. Then more people pointed at Brynn.

Brynn's heart began to race. She wished that she

wasn't alone, and that Will or Jade or even Priscilla were with her. There was no reason to think that anyone meant Brynn harm. But still, she found herself tightly gripping the straps of her backpack as she continued on her way.

Then, as she swam past the large courthouse, she saw the dagon Ian Fletcher.

Ian Fletcher! He was the dagon who worked for Phaedra. The dagon who'd taken her pet turtle Tully and made him into a work turtle. The dagon who'd done nothing but helped to make Brynn's life miserable.

What is he doing here? Brynn thought. *As if I need more problems in my life, Ian Fletcher shows up in my very own neighborhood!*

To her alarm, Ian saw Brynn and promptly swam directly toward her. Hoping it was a coincidence, Brynn adjusted her path, swimming out of the way of the dagon. But Ian moved as well, his eyes locked on her.

He swam right in front of her, blocking her path.

"How does it feel?" he asked.

"What?" Brynn said.

"How does it feel to be responsible for the imprisonment of an innocent sea witch?"

Brynn tried to swim around the dagon, but he wouldn't let her.

"Leave me alone," said Brynn. "What are you doing here, anyway?"

"We're all waiting to see if Phaedra is going to be released. The court is in recess at the moment, but she's going to go free, you know. She's going to be found innocent, and then *you're* going to pay."

Ian gave her a small shove.

"Stop it!" said Brynn, moving backwards.

"And that's not all," hissed Ian. "Things are going to be very different around here very soon. Gone are the days when people are persecuted for guarding the ocean from those terrible humans."

Ian and the sea witch were just a few of a growing number of ocean residents who had decided humans were responsible for the majority of trouble under the sea—pollution, litter, over-fishing, and oil spills were all the doing of humans, and many seafolk, Phaedra included, thought that the humans ought to be punished.

It was true that humans caused major problems for the creatures living beneath the sea. Phaedra, Ian, and others believed the solution was to rid the ocean of humans through whatever means possible. Others, including Brynn and her parents, believed that harming humans would be a violation of the mermaid oath: *A merperson is a protector of the ocean, a guardian of the sea. Wherever living things need help, that's where we'll be.* That's why Brynn had helped to stop Phaedra from harming the humans. Humans were living beings, too.

Ian moved toward Brynn with his teeth bared and a menacing look in his eyes.

"You stay away from me," yelled Brynn.

There were a few mer-police officers around, and to Brynn's great relief, one of them must have heard Brynn yelling at Ian. The officer swam over to Brynn and Ian. This officer was a big, bulky merman with a gigantic tail and a flowing beard. Brynn recognized him at once as Officer McScales. He was one of the officers Brynn had worked with recently to apprehend the sea witch.

"Leave her alone, Ian," said Officer McScales.

Ian scowled at the mer-police officer.

"In fact," said McScales, "if you're gonna make trouble around here, why don't you just go on home."

Ian squinted at Brynn. "Soon, little mermaid, soon," he hissed.

"If you've got something to tell her, why don't you speak up, Fletcher," said Officer McScales.

But Ian skulked away, looking back over his shoulder.

Brynn felt as though she could hardly breathe. As soon as Ian swam off, Officer McScales turned to her.

"Are you all right?" he asked.

Brynn nodded. "What was he doing here? What are all these people doing here? Is Phaedra really going to be released from jail?"

"The sea witch's trial has gotten a lot of interest from people. They've come to watch. But I don't want you to worry. The mer-police knows about Ian's involvement with the sea witch. We've been looking out for you. For the next little bit we're going to have officers stationed all around here and if you need help, all you'll have to do is shout. Do you understand?"

"Yes, sir," said Brynn. Having Ian threaten her like that had really scared Brynn, but she felt a little bit safer knowing that the mer-police were looking out for her. Why did the sea witch have to be so troublesome?

When Brynn got home, she told her parents what had happened with Ian, and they were both quite upset.

"Hey," her mother asked, "how come you weren't with Jade?"

Brynn couldn't hold in her emotions anymore. When her mother asked about Jade, Brynn was reminded of her crumbling friendship with Jade, and her shoulders slumped.

"I don't think Jade wants to be my friend anymore."

Brynn's parents looked at each other. They hated seeing their daughter struggle with friendships and wished that they could do something to help.

"Brynn, I know it's really hard right now, but I

went through something like this when I was your age, too," said her mom. "I had a group of friends and for some reason, at some point, they just decided they didn't want to be friends with me anymore. They stopped inviting me to do things and then they started horrible rumors about me at school. It was awful!"

Brynn swallowed hard. It was true that Priscilla and Jade were doing things without her, but they hadn't been spreading rumors about her. Was that coming next? She wouldn't even want to go to school if they started doing that.

"What did you do?" Brynn asked.

"Well, at first I tried to keep on being friends with them. I'd invite them over, or invite them to do things with me, but they always said no. If I heard they were doing something together without me, I'd try to get myself invited. I even begged my mom to tell their moms to let me hang out. Can you guess how that went over?"

"What happened?" asked Brynn.

"Well, my mom and their moms made arrangements for me to come to sleep over, but it wasn't fun at all. They whispered about me right in front of me, and they weren't very nice."

It was hard for Brynn to imagine her mother being treated poorly. Her mom was so cool and smart and fun. Why would anyone ever be mean to her?

"So then what?" Brynn asked.

"Eventually, I realized that I didn't want to be friends with people who would treat me that way. I tried to get them to stop spreading rumors about me. I yelled at them, and I called them liars."

"And that stopped them?"

"I wish. If anything, that only made things worse," said Dana.

"This type of behavior is a form of bullying," said Brynn's father. "Exclusion, spreading rumors, and things like that might not leave bruises, but they still hurt."

"So you're saying Jade and Priscilla are bullying me?" Brynn asked.

"I don't think so," said Adrian. "But sometimes friendships just change for reasons we don't understand. People and relationships change, and that's not bullying. But shunning, name-calling, rumor-spreading—that's bullying."

"I don't think they are trying to hurt me on purpose," said Brynn. "They haven't been purposely mean or anything—it's like they're always just busy doing stuff together without me."

"Jade's always been into singing," Adrian point out, "so it's nice that she has a friend now who enjoys it as much as she does. Maybe it's a temporary thing."

"So, what did you do about the friends who were being so mean to you, Mom?" Brynn asked.

"Well, at first I thought it was my fault," said

Dana. "I thought the bad things they said about me were true. But then I realized that I wasn't a bad person, and that I had many good qualities. After that, it was easier to withstand the rumors. I knew who I really was. I knew I was a good and valuable mermaid. And the people who knew me best—the people who mattered, like my family— they knew the truth about who I really was. It doesn't matter what other people say about you, if you know your own truth. I think those other mermaids eventually got bored of spreading rumors because they were no longer getting a reaction out of me. And because of that experience, I made new friends—better friends—who would stick with me through thick or thin. They're still my friends today, but I never would have made those lifelong friends if I'd still been trying to make things work with those original mermaids."

"Wowee," said Brynn. She scratched her head. "So, what do you think I should do, exactly? Should I stop trying to be Jade's friend?"

"I'm not saying that," said Dana. "I'm just telling you to remember who you really are and to know that there are plenty of mermaids in the sea who would love to be your friend. I hope things work out between you and Jade and even Priscilla, but if they don't, you'll be okay. No matter what happens, you have your dad and me on your side."

"Always," said Adrian. "There's nothing that could change that."

Just then Tully nudged Brynn with his head.

Adrian laughed. "I think Tully is saying he's on your side, too, Brynn. And I'm sure you can think of others you can count on—other friends, teachers, and your grandparents."

Brynn nodded. Will was still a good friend and he was lots of fun. And she knew she could always count on her magic teacher, Ms. Meyers. Her grandparents lived far away, but she still knew they loved her. She might be without Jade, but she wasn't alone.

It was shocking to hear that her mom had friend troubles when she was in middle grade, and Brynn wondered how common it was. Were there other mermaids at Crystal Water Middle School having the same problem?

Adrian and Dana said they'd pick up Brynn after school for the next little while, to ensure she wouldn't have any more trouble with the newcomers to town, but Brynn begged them not to.

"No one else has their parents picking them up. Besides, Officer McScales said the mer-police were going to be sticking around the neighborhood and they'd look out for me."

Her parents hadn't liked it, but they reluctantly agreed.

"Come straight home after school then," said Dana. "And if anyone bothers you, yell for help."

Brynn took Tully outside for his visit to the surface and while she did, she thought about her friendship with Jade. They had so many memories together.

Brynn sighed. She wasn't ready to give up on their friendship just yet.

CHAPTER NINE

*L*ater that day, Brynn did something that always made her feel better. She swam to the kelp forest. There, among the closely spaced waving stalks of dark-green kelp, was a clearing where the sun beamed peacefully down. It was a great place to relax, think, and practice magic. It was one of Brynn's special undersea spots, a place where she could escape to when things weren't going well.

The encounter with Ian Fletcher had been a bit scary, but Brynn was actually more upset about her friendship with Jade and the way it was changing. Jade and Brynn had been friends since before they could even swim, and Brynn could not recall their relationship ever being so out of sorts. Things were different between them now in a way that it never had been before. Even when Mrs. Sands forbade the two mermaids from seeing each other, Brynn had known in her heart that they were still best friends. Now Brynn wasn't sure if they were even friends at all, let alone best friends.

Brynn sighed and raised her eyes to the tops of the kelp strands. As they moved on the waves at the ocean's surface, the sunlight broke through and shimmered like magic. The view from Brynn's rock in the forest was ever-changing, always different.

Brynn decided again that, rather than worry about it on her own, she should just talk honestly with Jade about how she felt. She swam home from the kelp forest as the sun was setting and it was getting dark. The peaceful kelp and the warm sun had cleared her mind, and she felt ready to try again to repair her troubled friendship.

Jade hadn't been riding the speed-current anymore—instead, Priscilla's family gave her a ride to and from school each day. So, the next day, when Brynn got to school, she looked for Jade. She spotted Jade in the noisy and crowded hallway and swam up to her.

"Jade," she said, "can I talk to you?"

"Sure," said Jade with an edge of hesitation in her voice.

Brynn knew that Jade was probably remembering what happened last time they'd met up in the hallways at school, but Brynn had decided to remain calm and friendly.

"What's up?" said Jade nervously.

Brynn took a deep breath. "Well, the last time we spoke, it seemed like maybe we weren't friends anymore. Is that really how you feel?"

Jade took a deep breath. "No, Brynn. I was just mad because it felt like you were trying to keep me from hanging out with Priscilla. We're definitely still friends."

"That's good. But we never see each other anymore. And during the time we used to spend together—like in the morning waiting for the speed-current, and playing Mermies at my house—you're usually with Priscilla." It was difficult to say such things without crying or getting angry, but Brynn tried really hard. "It seems like you don't have much time for me lately."

"It's not that," said Jade. "It's just that I really love singing and Priscilla does, too, and I know that singing's not really your thing."

"So that's it? It's just about the singing?"

"Yeah," said Jade. "She's a great singer, and we have lots of fun singing together."

Brynn thought maybe she'd been wrong about this whole drama. Will and Brynn's parents had been trying to tell her that everything would be all right. Had Brynn just been over-reacting? She thought back about her interactions with Priscilla. Brynn had been envious and sarcastic.

"I still like you, Brynn. A lot. We've been best friends forever."

"I know," said Brynn. "But it just seems so different now."

The bell rang and Brynn sighed. She wanted to keep talking until she felt better.

"We better go," said Jade. "I don't want to be late for class."

But something Jade had said gave Brynn an idea. So, that afternoon after school let out, Brynn swam to the choral music room to speak with Cecilia Blue, the music teacher who taught choir.

"Hi, Ms. Blue," said Brynn. "I was wondering if maybe you could give me some private singing lessons. I could use my allowance to pay you."

Ms. Blue smiled. "I do indeed provide private lessons. Why the sudden interest?"

"Well, it's not so much that my interest has increased —" Brynn hesitated, wondering if she should be upfront about the real reason she was asking for lessons.

Ms. Blue had always been a nice teacher. She was one of the oldest teachers at Crystal Water Middle School, but Brynn noticed that the wrinkles at her eyes and on her forehead were all turned up instead of down, which Brynn was certain was a result from years of smiling. In fact, Ms. Blue reminded Brynn of an older version of her favorite teacher—Windy Meyers, who taught Beginning Magic. And this resemblance made her think that she could trust Ms. Blue with even her deepest secrets.

"To be honest," Brynn began. "I still don't really care much about singing, sorry to say, but Jade has been hanging out a lot with Priscilla Banks because they are both into singing, and while that's great and everything, what I'd really like is for Jade to hang out more with me, and it's fine if Priscilla wants to come along, too, I just don't want to be left out, but the last time we all went to sing, I was kinda loud and maybe a little bit off key, and I broke their Swymbits, so I thought I should probably get better at singing, and if I become a better singer then maybe they'd like me more."

Ms. Blue inhaled. "I see. My, that was quite a lot of information."

"Yeah, so you can see why I need to improve my singing."

"If you really want lessons, I'm happy to give them to you, but Brynn, friends don't have to like all the same things. We're all different from each other. It's our uniqueness that makes us special and makes us interesting to other people. It wouldn't be a very nice place if everyone thought and acted exactly the same. Your singing might not be the best, but you have other talents that make you special. Mrs. Meyers tells me all the time what a talented mergician you are. She says you have a real gift for magic."

Brynn's heart swelled at the thought of her

favorite teacher giving her such praise. "She really said that?"

"Mm-hm. And from watching you, I know there are two things you really enjoy doing and neither of them are singing. Do you know what I'm thinking of?"

"Magic and dancing?"

"That's right. So are you really sure you want to spend your time and money on private singing lessons?"

Brynn thought about this. There were a lot of other things she could spend her sand dollars on, and she couldn't see herself getting excited over the singing lessons. But on the other hand, Jade was around less and less.

"Yes," said Brynn. "If you wouldn't mind, I'd still like to take the lessons."

"All right then," said Ms. Blue. "How about we start next week?"

While Brynn wasn't particularly excited about the singing lessons, the thought of improving her singing made her feel like she was in control of the friendship situation.

I'll become a better singer, and ask Jade to practice with me, and we'll become best friends again. Bubble-bing, bubble-boom, thought Brynn.

The thought of it had put her in a good mood, and she was excited to share this possible solution with her parents, so she practically burst through the front door of her sea cave.

"Mom, Dad, I'm home! You'll never guess what I decided to do today!"

Brynn spotted both her parents in the living room and swam toward them. But she could instantly tell something was wrong. Their faces were pale, and they were holding each other.

Brynn's stomach fell. She said, "What is it?" but she knew it must have something to do with Phaedra the sea witch.

CHAPTER TEN

*A*fter Phaedra had been captured, Brynn had assumed that would be the end of her sea-witch troubles. After all, Phaedra's attempts to harm humans was strictly against the mermaid oath, which declared: *A merperson is a protector of the ocean, a guardian of the sea. Wherever living things need help, that's where we'll be.*

But even for non-merfolk like the sea witch, who didn't believe in the mermaid oath, all the living creatures in the ocean were subject to the prevailing laws. These had been jointly agreed upon by the Undersea Peace Council, and one of those laws forbade interaction with the humans, and it especially forbade causing them any harm.

The mer-authorities were well aware of Phaedra's abilities, so while she was under arrest, they'd be sure to make certain that Phaedra wouldn't be able to cast any of her magical spells. Further, they had plenty of evidence and witnesses to show that Phaedra had intentionally tried to harm the humans. So, in Brynn's mind, once Phaedra was arrested, it was only a matter of time before she was sent to jail.

"I don't understand," Brynn said to her parents. "What do you mean she's been released?"

Never before had Adrian and Dana, Brynn's parents, wore such strained expressions.

"It's been on the news," said Dana, gesturing at the shell-a-vision. "Judge Waterly said that not only was Phaedra not guilty of any crime, but that she should be applauded for her efforts to protect the ocean from the humans."

"What?" said Brynn. It was like her parents were speaking some unknown language.

"It was so unexpected," said Adrian, nodding, then shaking his head, then nodding again. "Judge Waterly has been an ardent supporter of the merfolk oath. In the past, he has held a firm stance on protecting the humans and not causing them any harm, even when some of them had caused harm to the ocean."

Brynn dropped her book bag. *This can't be happening*, she thought. She flipped on the shell-a-vision.

The screen immediately filled with the image of Phaedra the sea witch leaving the courthouse, her perfect red lips curled into a winning smile as she waved and blew kisses to the cameras and reporters.

"So that's it?" Brynn asked. "They're just letting her go?"

Adrian nodded. "She was found not guilty. They have to release her."

"But she *is* guilty!" Brynn said, womping the floor with her tail. "She tried to sink those ships. I saw it with my own eyes!"

"Sometimes things happen in life that aren't right or fair," said Dana.

"But why?" asked Brynn.

"I don't know," said Dana. "It's really frustrating when things turn out this way. We just have to keep doing our best and follow what we know to be right in our hearts."

On the shell-a-vision, the camera turned to a merman in front of the building. He was a tall merman and he wore a brown suit and tie and had thick glasses.

"Not only was my client not guilty," said the mer, looking into the camera with a stern expression, "but we feel the anti-human-harm law is antiquated and wrong. We aren't going to stop now that Phaedra has been released. We're going to keep fighting until this law is overturned."

"What does that mean?" Brynn asked.

"It means they want to get rid of the law that keeps the undersea folk in the ocean from harming humans. They want to make it so it is not illegal to punish and hurt the humans. Basically, they want to make Phaedra's actions legal. Like when she tried to sink those ships and hurt all those people," said Adrian.

"But wouldn't that go against the merfolk oath?" Brynn asked.

"I think so," said Dana. "The merfolk oath is about protecting others. It refers to 'living beings.' I don't know how you can exclude the humans as living beings. Even if they don't live in the ocean, and even if they're clumsy and reckless with their garbage and pollution."

"Who is that merman?" Brynn asked.

"It's Phaedra's lawyer," said Adrian. "He was hired to defend the sea witch against the charges, and now he's trying to get the anti-human-harm law changed."

"But surely they won't change the law!" Brynn cried.

"I can't imagine they will," said Adrian. "But that doesn't mean they won't try."

Brynn couldn't imagine how they could try to get rid of laws that protected living beings. It went against everything merfolk believed in.

"Why would anyone want to harm the humans?" Brynn asked. "I don't understand."

Adrian sighed. "It's complicated, Brynn. Some would say that the humans are causing harm to those of us who live in the ocean. Not all of them, but some of them, *are* doing things that can hurt ocean life. Things like throwing trash in the ocean and oil spills and overfishing. That can cause a lot of plants and animals in the ocean to die."

"But hurting the humans won't make it right!" said Brynn.

"I agree with you," said Adrian. "But that's not how everyone feels. A lot of people are fed up, and they want to send the humans a message."

Brynn looked back to the shell-a-vision. Phaedra's lawyer was still talking about teaching the humans a harsh lesson. He was talking about ridding the oceans of all humans. And then Brynn noticed something.

The lawyer was wearing a Swymbit.

It wasn't covered in sparkles, though. It was more business-like—plain gray and silver. Brynn had only noticed it because it made a bright green flash that caught her eye.

That figures, thought Brynn. It seemed to her that everyone who wore one of those ridiculous Swymbits was annoying or upsetting to her in some way.

The scene on the shell-a-vision changed to recorded video of the Honorable Matthew Waterly delivering his verdict. Brynn watched as the judge reached out to tap the bench with his gavel, the small wooden hammer that all judges used to make their decisions final.

But as the judge's black robes swept back from his hand, Brynn noticed that he was wearing a Swymbit, too! The judge's model was plain black, like his robes, and again Brynn would not have seen it if it hadn't flashed green for an instant.

Ugh, thought Brynn, *not him, too! This is like some kind of ocean-wide conspiracy!*

Almost all the teachers and students at school had Swymbits now. Brynn was starting to feel like she was the only person in the whole school without one.

Now the scene on the shell-a-vision switched to show Phaedra. She stood in front of the courthouse, surrounded by reporters and answering questions.

"Yes," she said, "I'm very pleased with the verdict. It's very fair, and it's very wise, and it will allow me to pursue my intentions of ridding the oceans of the wicked influence of the humans—" here she paused to look right into the camera, and she added "—and others who might try to interfere."

Brynn knew Phaedra had meant that last comment just for her, or at least she thought it was. Phaedra may have been using some kind of magic, or perhaps it was only her agitated mind.

She'll never give up until she's turned me into a sea slug! thought Brynn.

Just then, a subtle flash on the shell-a-vision caught Brynn's eye. As the sea witch raised her hand to sweep back her lovely jet-black hair, something on her wrist flashed.

Another Swymbit! This one was fit for someone like Phaedra—it sparkled with fabulous sea jewels and was contoured to complement the sea witch's long, beautiful limbs. But the thing that Brynn found very interesting was that Phaedra's Swymbit flashed red. All the others she'd seen were flashing green.

Weird, thought Brynn.

Nevertheless, Brynn immediately flipped the shell-a-vision off. It just reminded her of the things that were bothering her the most at the moment: Swymbits and the sea witch.

"So what does this mean for me?" Brynn asked, turning to her parents. She was thinking of what Ian had said the other day by the courthouse—about how the sea witch was going to go free and make Brynn pay.

Adrian and Dana looked at each other as though each hoped the other one had a good answer. That's when Brynn realized that maybe her parents didn't know what to do. It frightened her to think that there were things in the world that her parents couldn't handle.

"Brynn, we're going to have to be careful again," said Dana. "We know the sea witch is angry with you, but hopefully she'll be busy enough with these other interests that she doesn't come looking for you. But just in case, we've asked the mer-police to keep an eye out for the next little bit."

Brynn nodded. She remembered how Officer

McScales had helped her out that day at the courthouse, and it made her feel a bit better knowing they'd be looking out for her.

"If you ever feel like you are in any danger, always ask for help," said Dana. "There will always be someone who believes in the merfolk oath and who will come to your aid."

The older Brynn had gotten, the more she realized how complicated the world was. Not even adults could agree on what was right or wrong, best or worst, but Brynn believed in the merfolk oath with her whole heart, and she believed that if she and others followed it, they could never go wrong.

CHAPTER ELEVEN

The next day, Brynn awoke with a strange feeling. She felt that something big was about to happen. Was it something about the water filtered down from the breaking waves above? Or was there a special electricity in the water itself? Brynn couldn't say, and of course she didn't know what might happen—if anything.

And so she went through the motions of her morning routine—brushing her teeth, styling her hair, getting dressed, taking Tully to the surface, eating breakfast—but she was barely aware she was doing any of it.

She had little reason to think anything would improve. And so she left her house for the speed-current stop in a sort of daze, thinking that the day would more than likely be just as drab and sad as the rest of the week had been. She spoke to no one and took no notice of anything. She went from class to class robotically, but she peeked around each corner and peered into each shadow with a weird combination of suspicion and curiosity.

One class melted into the next, lunch came and went, and soon it was time for the school pep rally. Crystal Water Middle School's swim team was getting ready for a big meet with their longtime rival, Blue Wave Middle School. It was the Crystal Water Manta Rays against the Blue Wave Dolphins, and the entire school was exuberantly excited for the contest.

Everyone but Brynn, of course. She didn't so much "go" to the pep rally as drift along the halls, carried by the current and flow of the other students as they gathered in the gym.

The rivalry between the two schools was always a big deal, but this year both schools had excellent teams, and there was simply no way to know which school would prevail. Accordingly, there was much interest in the upcoming swim meet, and so the gym was rapidly filling with students.

Brynn found what she figured must be the last unclaimed seat in the bleachers, but then she only sat there looking down at her tail fin while the other students cheered and shouted. When the members of the swim team entered the gym, the students got even louder, hollering and stamping their tails. Brynn looked up to watch them come in. The swimmers held up their hands and pumped their fists, as though they had already won the swim meet. The cheer-leaders were leading the crowd in some cheer chants.

Sea! Aggressive! Sea! Sea! Aggressive!

Go! Fight! Swim! Go! Fight! Swim!

When we say Manta, you say Rays! Manta! Rays! Manta! Rays!

Ordinarily, Brynn would have joined in. She was very proud of the Crystal Water Manta Rays and their many championships. She loved pep rallies and swim meets, and she always sang along and clapped and stamped her tail fin.

This time, however, Brynn watched the pep rally with a bored expression.

Then, however, she spotted a familiar sight—the long and gleaming white hair of her best friend. Jade was sitting in the bleachers, too, about nine or ten rows down from Brynn. She was clapping along to the sports chants.

But the thing that really caught Brynn's eye was that Jade was by herself. Priscilla wasn't around. And not only that—amazingly, there was a vacant seat next to Jade.

Brynn thought for what seemed like a long time about what to do. Lately, every time she had tried to talk to Jade, it'd seemed wrong in some way. Things between the two mermaids were bad enough already, Brynn knew, and she wasn't eager to make them worse. And so she turned the problem over in her mind for several minutes as the pep rally thundered in the gym.

It probably would have been best to just let sleeping dogfish lie, Brynn thought, but she couldn't help herself. This felt like a sign of some sort, and so she swam down the bleachers, nudging her way through the jostling merkids. She quietly swam to where Jade was seated. Then, utterly silent, she scooted into the seat next to Jade.

And then Brynn did nothing. Nothing at all.

Jade did not notice Brynn, and Brynn for her part sat like a terrified statue. A grin of terrible nervousness had appeared on her face, but she said and did nothing to attract Jade's attention. Jade went on clapping her hands and chanting along with the cheerleaders, totally engrossed in school spirit and encouraging the swim team. The merkids all around them did the same, allowing Brynn to remain practically invisible.

This went on for several minutes. Brynn thought about saying something or tapping Jade on the shoulder. But she thought that might break the spell or something. Brynn wasn't talking and cheering with Jade, but this way she was at least *with* Jade. If she got Jade's attention, Brynn thought Jade might go and sit somewhere else. Or worse—Priscilla might show up.

And so Brynn stayed quiet, possibly the only

mermaid in the entire school who was doing that at the moment.

But of course that couldn't last—you can't really sit right next to someone without them noticing you eventually, not even in the noise and excitement of a pep rally.

The cheerleaders started "the wave" in the gym, where the merkids on one side of the gym jumped up in their seat and waved their arms, followed by the merkids next to them and so on, mimicking a wave that flows across the whole crowd. Merkids were especially good at the wave, of course, because they could actually float up from their seats, making their waves very dramatic and smooth—very like real ocean waves.

But it was at this moment that Jade noticed Brynn. As the wave came along the bleachers, Jade leaped up from her seat, raised her arms and as she turned to watch the wave continue on, she saw Brynn.

"Oh. Hi, Brynn," said Jade with a smile.

"Hi, Jade!" said Brynn. She was still wearing her super-nervous grin.

"How long have you been sitting there?" asked Jade with a surprised chuckle. "I didn't even notice you!"

You can say that again, Brynn thought. *You haven't noticed me hardly at all ever since Priscilla showed up!*

She didn't say anything like that to Jade, of course.

Instead, she grinned even more and said, "Oh, yeah! Wowee! I guess I didn't notice you there, either! What a funny coincidence! We just show up on the same row at the pep rally, and we don't even notice, and so now here we are sitting next to each other! Gee, I hope the Manta Rays beat the Dolphins!" Brynn was smiling so hard she thought her face might crack.

"Oh, they will. We have the most fin-tastic team in the sea this year," replied Jade.

"So, um, hey, huh, I just realized something!" said Brynn, trying to sound casual but doing a very bad job at it.

"What's that?" asked Jade, and she really did sound casual.

"Well, I mean, uhm, I happened to notice, you know, that you're not with Priscilla," said Brynn.

"Yeah," said Jade, a sudden nervousness now in her voice, "that's the thing that's so weird."

"Weird?" asked Brynn.

"Yes, weird," answered Jade, and in her voice was that tone one uses when something embarrassing has happened. "Because, see, that's why I'm sitting here and why I didn't think you'd be sitting there—I was saving this seat for Priscilla."

"Oooh," said Brynn. Her face flushed red and she laughed, but not because she thought something was funny. "Riiight," she continued. "*That's* why this seat was empty."

"Uh huh," said Jade. "And, uhm, please don't be upset, Brynn, but, well, Priscilla's here now."

Priscilla had come up behind Brynn. She tapped Brynn on the shoulder and said, "Hi!"

Brynn jumped as if stung by a jelly fish and turned around to face Priscilla.

"Well," said Priscilla, "this is awkward."

"Hmm?" said Brynn, raising her eyebrows. "Awkward? No! No, no, no." She turned back to Jade. "Didn't I mention, Jade? I've got to be going!"

"Going?" asked Jade. "Going where?"

"To a meeting, of course," Brynn replied.

Jade and Priscilla both frowned with confusion at this.

"Brynn, what are you talking about? What kind of meeting? The whole school is here."

"It's, uhm, a special meeting," Brynn managed to say. "A club meeting. Yes. For a club I'm in."

Jade raised a skeptical eyebrow. "I didn't know you were in a club."

"Oh," Brynn stuttered. "That's because I just joined it, recently. Today."

"What kind of club is it?" asked Jade, folding her arms.

"What kind of club is it?" Brynn repeated, her mind racing. "Why, a friendship club, of course."

"Uh huh," scoffed Jade. "And they're having a meeting right now."

"Yes," said Brynn.

"During the biggest pep rally of the year."

"It was an unfortunate scheduling decision, but yes," said Brynn.

"Well, fine," said Jade. "See you around."

Brynn swam off as fast as her tail fin could manage. She even thought of casting a speed spell on herself, but soon she was outside the gym and she breathed a big sigh of relief. Still, her face was red and she felt awful. She wanted nothing more than to put the whole terrible business behind her, so she headed straight for the speed-current stop.

Just as she'd been at school, Brynn again fell into a daze as the speed-current carried her to her neighborhood. It still felt as though something major were about to happen, but what? Could she possibly make things worse with Jade? What was this feeling she had? As Brynn hopped off the speed-current, she assumed she was just being silly.

CHAPTER TWELVE

*E*ven though Brynn didn't really have a club meeting that afternoon, she did have somewhere to be after the pep rally. It was her third day of singing lessons with Ms. Blue.

"Now, sit up straight, lift your chin, and take a deep breath," said Ms. Blue.

I can't believe I spent my allowance on singing lessons, thought Brynn.

"Let's practice some scales," said Ms. Blue. She played a chord on her sea-ano.

I could have bought some new Mermies with that money.

"Watch your pitch, Brynn. Pay attention." She tapped a few times on the key of the sea-ano until Brynn sang the right note.

I don't see what Jade and Priscilla love so much about singing. I'd much rather be dancing.

"Fa-la-la-la-la,'" instructed Ms. Blue, playing the notes of the scale.

"Fa-la-la-la-la," sang Brynn.

"Enunciate, dear. La-la-la," sang Ms. Blue, enunciating each syllable. "And don't forget your posture. And let's have some enthusiasm, too. Right now it almost sounds like you're singing against your will." Ms. Blue chuckled.

Brynn sighed. *If you only knew,* she thought, trying to enunciate, sit up straight, lift her chin and breathe from her diaphragm—all at the same time.

"Fa-la-la-la-la-la-la!" sang Brynn.

"Better," said Ms. Blue, nodding her head.

Brynn stopped singing and said, "Couldn't we sing some fun songs, like Jay Barracuda's music? Why do we have to do all these scales?"

"These are voice exercises. They'll make you a stronger singer. If you just want to jam out to music for a while, that's fine, but you told me you wanted lessons to become a better singer," said Ms. Blue.

"Yeah, I guess so," said Brynn.

"Brynn, a mermaid singing is a magical thing. *Literally* magical. It can enhance spells, and when voices sing in harmony, the songs can create their own magic. But it isn't something you can do half-heartedly. You have to commit to exercising and practicing. It has to be something you really desire."

"Okay," said Brynn.

Now it was Ms. Blue who stopped. She took her

hands off the sea-ano keys and said, "I could be wrong, Brynn, but I'm getting the impression that you're not really enjoying these lessons and that you're having second thoughts. Am I wrong?"

Brynn sighed. "No, you're not wrong."

"When we talked about doing the lessons, you told me it was because you were having a little friend trouble," said Ms. Blue. "And you wanted to get better at singing to improve that situation?"

"Yes." Brynn nodded. "If I could get as good at singing as they are, then they won't go to Mammoth Cave without inviting me."

"It is true that we sometimes need to do things for friends. For example, we need to take turns picking activities to do with friends, and your friend might pick something that you don't really enjoy. And that's okay. Friendship is about being flexible, like kelp, you bend and sway so that you're a good fit for each other and both make life better for one another. But friendship isn't about changing who you are as a person. Do you understand?"

"I'm not sure," said Brynn.

"If there's something you hate doing or something you don't agree with, you shouldn't do it just for the sake of friendship. You have to be true to yourself, too."

"So, you're saying I shouldn't take singing lessons just to get my friend back?"

"I'm saying you should only take singing lessons"

if it is what your heart desires. If you're not enjoying it, then do something you love instead. Good friends will want to see you doing things that make you happy, not doing things just to impress them."

"Ms. Blue?"

"Yes?"

"You're a really good teacher. Not just for the singing, but with other stuff, too, like teaching about friendships. Will you be upset if I quit the lessons?"

"No, I won't be upset, but I will miss seeing you."

"Maybe I could stop by to say 'hi' sometimes."

"Sure," said Ms. Blue.

"And maybe, just for fun, we could sing something besides fa-la-la."

Ms. Blue laughed. "I do like me some Jay Barracuda," she said.

And with that, Brynn finished her after-school singing lessons. She resolved herself to knowing that she would never be as good of a singer as Jade or Priscilla. And that probably meant that they would keep going to Mammoth Cave without her. Brynn tried and tried to think of a way to save her friendship. But friendships are a funny thing. If you try to force them, they don't work. This is what Brynn was thinking about when she swam up to her friend's house and knocked on the door.

Will answered the door. "Hey, Brynn, what's up?"

"I just wondered," said Brynn, "if you maybe wanted to hang out, or go for a swim, or go for a swim and then hang out, or hang out first and then go for a swim. Or something."

"Sure," said Will. "Why so glum? Still having friendship drama?"

"Oh, I don't know," said Brynn, staring at the doormat on Will's front porch. "Is it all right if we don't talk about that right now?"

"Yes," said Will. "Thank goodness. Cuz, I don't want to hear about it."

Brynn put her hands on her hips. "William Beach! What an awful thing to say!"

Will shrugged with a bit more snark than usual. "Hey, it was your idea. In fact, let's make it official. No talking about Brynn's friend problems for the rest of this whole day." He put his hand out. "Let's shake on it."

Brynn laughed a little. Then she shook his hand. "But how'd you know it was friend problems?"

"Brynn, you *always* have friend problems," said Will with a grin. "But you don't have a problem with me. So, come on in. Wanna listen to some music?"

To Brynn, listening to music seemed like the perfect thing. It wouldn't require talking or even thinking.

"Actually, that sounds wonderful," said Brynn. "Thanks, Will."

Will turned on the music. Something told him the volume needed to be not too loud, but not too quiet, either. The two merkids didn't dance or sing, and they didn't even talk very much. Will lay on his bed, reading a comic book. Brynn sat in a chair braiding lengths of her lavender hair, then unbraiding them, then starting over.

If someone had looked in on them, it might have appeared that they weren't having any fun at all. But Brynn was truly enjoying herself. Being in a different place with the music playing allowed Brynn to forget her troubles for a while. Will didn't even seem to know she was there. He didn't ask her about her problems. He didn't ask her about anything.

Every now and then, Brynn would say, "Oh, I love this song."

And Will would turn it up a little.

Or Brynn would say, "This one's kinda sad."

And Will would nod and turn the page of his comic book.

Will kept the music playing until they'd listened to practically every song Jay Barracuda and the Killer Whales had ever recorded. Soon Will had read almost every comic book he owned, too.

After a long afternoon, Brynn unbraided her hair, sighed, and said, "Hey, Will?"

"What's up?" answered Will, looking up from the latest issue of Crab-Man.

"Thanks," said Brynn softly.

"You're welcome," said Will. "Thank you for what?"

"For just letting me be here and not expecting me to be interesting or talkative."

"Oh," said Will with a snarky eye-roll. "I'm pretty sure you'll be talkative if I ever need you to be."

He smiled, and Brynn knew he was only kidding around. Will was good at that, and it always made her feel better.

"I think it's just what I needed," said Brynn.

"Don't forget that you're going to the Jay Barracuda show. You should look forward to that. You're gonna love it!"

"You've been to one of his shows?" asked Brynn.

"Yeah! His live shows are tubular! He's got lights and bubbles and a giant inflatable killer whale! You gotta get up close to the stage—all the band members come around and shake hands with the crowd. And make sure you get a t-shirt! And when they sing 'Swim to Me Again,' the crowd all swims in little circles. Ah, Brynn! You're gonna totally dig it!"

Brynn laughed. It seemed like maybe Will enjoyed even just the thought of her going to the concert.

"Oh!" cried Will. "Hey! Hang on!" He swam over to his dresser and rummaged in it for a while before he produced something small and round. "Here!" he said. "Wear this to the concert. Just don't lose it."

He held out a battered little badge that said JBATKW on it.

"Wowee! Did you get this at a show?"

"Yep," said Will. "It's one of my prized possessions. So, bring it back safe."

"Thanks, Will. This will go great with the jacket I was going to wear."

"Ooh, tell me what outfit you're going to wear. Wanna borrow my sunglasses?"

And so then they talked. They talked about JBATKW and concerts and outfits. It was growing late when Brynn realized she should get back home for dinner, and so she finally left. But for that afternoon, she had forgotten all about Jade and Priscilla, and if she were being honest, it felt really good.

CHAPTER THIRTEEN

*A*fter Brynn had dinner with her family that evening, Tully nudged Brynn's leg with his big beak.

"Wanna go for a little swim, boy?" asked Brynn, scratching Tully on his scaly head.

Tully smiled and narrowed his eyes.

Brynn got up from the couch and said, "I'm going to take Tully up to the surface."

Her father, Adrian, was at their dining room table, reading a cooking magazine. "Hey, I'll come with you," he said. "It'll be nice to stretch my fins. Dana, sweetheart, do you want to come?"

Brynn's mom, Dana, emerged from their bedroom. "Sure! It's such a pleasant evening."

It'd been a long time since the three of them had gone on a good long swim together. It was something

Brynn had enjoyed ever since she was little. But for whatever reason, they hadn't taken swims as a family very recently, so it was nice to get out with her parents for a change.

In the dusk, the water was a deep, dark blue, though there was still a golden light at the surface from the setting sun. They swam through the cool, refreshing water. Dana and Adrian held hands as they swam, while Brynn and Tully swam further ahead and then back to her parents again.

They reached the surface and while they waited for Tully to get some fresh air, they looked at the beautiful colors of the sunset. The sky was streaked with orange, purple, and pink.

Combined with the time she had spent with Will earlier in the day, it was almost enough to make her forget how much she missed Jade. Almost.

"Are you still excited for the Jay Barracuda concert next weekend?" Adrian asked Brynn as Tully paddled around her in the water.

"Of course," said Brynn. "I just found out that Will has gone to one of their concerts before with his mom and brother. He says it's a blast!"

When Tully finally seemed like he'd had enough of the surface, the Finley family began making their way back home.

But they were still a league or so from home when they saw a crowd of people and heard shouting.

"What's going on?" asked Brynn.

"I'm not sure," said Dana. "Let's take a look."

They swam closer to find a crowd of around twenty merpeople and dagons looking at a section of the coral reef.

While coral sometimes seemed like it was a plant, it was actually colonies of thousands of creatures who had hard outer skeletons of limestone all grown together. These creatures didn't move, but instead anchored themselves to rocks or the ocean floor.

Coral was usually brightly colored in shades like orange, teal, red, and pink, but the coral they had gathered around looked faded and gray.

A dagon jabbed a finger angrily at the coral. "Here's the proof," he shouted. "This coral is in terrible shape, and it's all because of the humans polluting the water. Something must be done! This cannot continue!"

Others in the crowd shouted their support.

Brynn wriggled through the crowd to get a better look.

The coral looked awful. It was pale and sickly.

"What's wrong with it?" Brynn asked her parents. "Why is it dying?"

Before Brynn's parents could respond, a merman with a long red beard and big bushy eyebrows turned to her. "I'll tell ya what's wrong," he said. "The humans are killin' the coral by changin' the water."

The merman pointed to the coral and Brynn realized that there were all kinds of debris trapped among the edges of the coral, too—plastic bags, all sorts of bottles, and discarded fishing gear.

Adrian swam close to Brynn. "All this trash in the ocean isn't great for the coral, but it is actually changes in the sea itself that causes this kind of damage to coral. The coral polyps are accustomed to certain ocean temperatures and specific water conditions. The humans are slowly changing our ocean's waters, and it's causing the coral to suffer."

"The sea witch was right," said a dagon with a high-pitched voice. "The humans must be stopped."

The crowd was restless and angry. Brynn could feel their hot energy, and she wondered if this had anything to do with what she'd been feeling earlier— that something was about to happen, that something big was coming. Anger crackled through the water as both merpeople and dagons and selkies alike observed the destruction of the coral reef.

"Can't we use mer-magic to heal it?" Brynn asked.

"We've tried," said a mermaid with thick spectacles. "Sometimes it works for a while, but most of the time, it doesn't. It's too far gone. Every day there is more and more damage to the reef. We can't keep up. There's not enough mer-magic in the all the seas to stop this amount of destruction."

Brynn looked to her parents, and they looked as

though they weren't sure what to think. Brynn herself understood that things in the ocean required a balance. The reef provided food and protection for hundreds of other species, and those species in turn helped hundreds of others. If the coral reef died completely, the effects to the ocean would be devastating, not to mention the harm it would cause to the peaceful little town of Fulgent.

A mermaid with cropped green hair shook her head. "The mermaid oath requires that we act. The coral is a living thing, and we must protect it!"

Then a dagon joined in, "We've got to keep these humans away from the oceans. Follow the example of the sea witch. Sink ships. Destroy piers. Do whatever we can to keep them far from the ocean!"

Brynn's mother spoke up, "What happened here isn't right, but we can't turn on the humans. If we harm them, we'll be no better than they are. We need to find a way to teach them—to show them what's happening under the water."

"Human lover," spat the dagon with the high voice.

Others in the crowd joined in. "Human lover," they murmured.

"Let's think about this rationally," said Adrian, swimming forward. He directed his attention to the merfolk. "Our oath is to protect all living things, and that includes the humans."

A few of the merpeople nodded their agreement,

but Adrian's words only seemed to make some of the other mers and seafolk even angrier.

"If you're not with us, you're against us," someone shouted.

"Please, we don't mean any trouble," said Dana.

"Someone needs to pay!" came another shout.

There was pushing in the crowds, more shouting. Fights were breaking out.

"I'm scared," said Brynn.

"Let's get out of here," said Adrian.

They swam away as the shouting and shoving around the coral reef increased.

Brynn's hands were shaking. What if the crowd had tried to hurt them? What if they had grown angrier? Back at home, Brynn's parents sent her to get ready for bed, but she overheard them talking in the kitchen.

"I don't understand what is happening," said Dana. "It isn't like merfolk to be so angry. It was almost like they were under the influence of some spell. Did you feel something strange?"

"Yes!" said Brynn's dad. "I have been feeling something odd now that you mention it. I've been feeling a strange anticipation in my mer-magic all day!"

Brynn stopped brushing her teeth, swam out of the bathroom, and hurried down the hall and into the kitchen.

"Ahf bwen fwulling thomthon woird, thoo!" cried Brynn. Flecks of toothpaste flew out of her mouth.

Her parents looked at her curiously.

"What's that, sweety?" asked Dana. "We can't understand you with your mouth all full of foam like that."

Brynn ran to the kitchen sink, washed her toothpaste down the drain, then repeated: "I've been feeling something weird, too!"

"Like a feeling of anticipation?" asked Adrian.

"Yeah!" replied Brynn excitedly.

"A feeling like something big is about to happen or change?" said Dana.

"Yes, yes!" said Brynn. "But I couldn't put my finger on it! I got up this morning and went through my morning routine, and I ate my breakfast and took Tully for a swim and got on the speed-current, and I just felt like something was going to happen but then nothing did happen, and I thought that was weird but then nothing kept happening and I thought I was just being silly but now something *is* happening! And you feel it, too!"

Brynn's parents chuckled. Then they traded a knowing look and nodded.

"This means you're developing stronger mer-magic," said Dana. "We cast spells with our mer-magic, but our magic can also tell us things. Sometimes it will tell us when something's wrong, or when something's going to happen that we need to pay attention to. This is good! Most merfolk have to be quite a bit older than you before they feel this intuition."

"Well, what's going to happen?" Brynn asked, barely able to contain herself. "What does it mean? What do we do now?"

"That's not clear," said Adrian, adjusting his glasses and rubbing his chin thoughtfully. "Your mother and I have been feeling it, too, but I'm not sure there's an answer, yet. Sometimes mer-magic is useful just to make you pay attention."

Brynn finished getting ready for bed, but after she and Tully curled up in her blankets, she found she couldn't sleep. What did it mean when even the adults didn't know what to do? She'd always assumed her parents knew what to do in every situation, but did this mean sometimes they didn't? Brynn didn't want to admit it, but she was worried. There were so many things that were wrong in the world, she wanted to fix it all, but she didn't know how. She wished she could go back to the days when her biggest problems were deciding what outfit to dress her Mermies in. She tossed and turned in her bed for hours trying to figure out what to do.

Brynn finally decided that all she could do was hold true to the merfolk oath: *A merperson is a protector of the ocean. A guardian of the sea. Wherever living things need help, that's where I'll be.*

"I have to protect the coral and the other marine

life, Tully," Brynn told her pet sea turtle. "It's part of the mer-oath, and that's what I'm meant to do with my life. But I've got to help the humans, too."

Comforted by the fact that she knew how she felt about it, Brynn finally fell asleep. But if she'd known what would happen over the next few days, she wouldn't have been able to sleep at all.

CHAPTER FOURTEEN

When Brynn woke up the next morning, her parents informed her that school had been cancelled for the day.

"Cancelled?" asked Brynn, still not quite awake yet. She glanced out the kitchen window. "How come? The weather looks nice. It's not a hurricane day, is it? Or is it a holiday? Is it Mer-morial Day already?"

"There's been more evidence of damaged coral. It's not just here in Fulgent. It's widespread. The Undersea Peace Council is holding an emergency meeting today to talk about the damage to the coral and the harm to other sea life that has been done," said Dana. "People are very upset about it, and the council knows that. They've cancelled school to allow everyone to listen and participate."

Brynn chewed the inside of her cheek. She was

thrilled that school was cancelled for the day, but something told her this wasn't good news.

"Are we going to go to the meeting and listen?" Brynn asked.

"After how angry that crowd got the other day," said Dana, "I think we better stay home and watch it unfold on the shell-a-vision."

"Agreed," said Adrian.

"Well, can I go play with my friends?" Brynn asked. Part of her was certain that Priscilla and Jade would be playing together. She was still determined to hang on to her friendship with Jade. But there was always Will to hang out with, too.

"Not today, Brynn. Today we're just going to stay home," said Adrian.

Brynn spent most of the day playing by herself in the room with her Mermies.

She made the white-haired Mermie that she called Shine swim over to the purple-haired Mermie called Rain.

"*Oh, I've missed you so much,*" Brynn said in a high-pitched voice as she bounced Shine back and forth.

"*Of course you have!*" Brynn waved Rain. "*Why ever did you leave me?*"

"*I was fooled by that other mermaid,*" Brynn made Shine say. "*I know now that she could never be as interesting and fun as you. I'm so sorry to have ever left you. Will you forgive me, daaahling?*"

"Of course, daaahling! But only on one condition. You must be my mermaid of honor at my wedding," said Rain.

"Why daaahling I'd be honored!" said Shine.

Brynn then spent a ridiculously long amount of time crafting a wedding dress out of seaweed paper and bits of other Mermies clothing, but only a small amount of time putting a bowtie on her Ben Mermie.

"Here swims the bride! Here swims the bride!" Brynn sang as she moved her Ben and Rain Mermies down an imaginary aisle.

When she got tired of playing with her Mermies, she swam out of her room to grab a snack.

Brynn had been in and out of her room all day. Each time, she found her parents watching the shell-a-vision.

Brynn would watch a little bit with them, but it all seemed very boring. It was just a bunch of mermen and mermaids in suits talking about regulations and treaties and agreements. Some stood at podiums and spoke, others sat in seats with their names on placards in front of them. All of them looked very bored.

Nothing about what they were saying was very interesting to Brynn. She heard the delegates mention some references to mer-history and there was lots of talk about the mer-oath. Some representatives from the dagons and selkies were there who talked to the assembly as well. To Brynn, this emergency meeting all seemed like a bunch of stuffy adult talk. She had noticed, too, that practically all of them were wearing

Swymbits, and that alone was enough to turn Brynn off from watching more.

But as Brynn was entering the living room, she saw that her parents were holding each other and their attention was completely focused on the meeting displayed on the shell-a-vision screen.

A very official looking mermaid, who was wearing glasses on the end of her nose, read from a document.

Oh, my oceans! thought Brynn, after seeing a little sea-lectronic green flash at the woman's wrist. *Even this lady has a Swymbit!*

The lady on the shell-a-vision began her statement. "Hereby, let it be known and let it be recorded that, effective immediately, by order of the Undersea Peace Council, the statutes pursuant to the Mer-human Interaction Act are hereby and forthwith withdrawn. Furthermore, let it be known that the council clarifies the mer-oath so that it pertains forthwith to creatures living *beneath* the sea, and the council advises those with mer-magical abilities to act accordingly. And let it be further-farther known to those who willingly, with or without knowledge, cause harm to the ocean and its inhabitants will be considered an enemy of the sea and permission is granted to take action in defense of the ocean. So let it be written. So let it be done."

Brynn's mother gasped while her father stared solemnly at the screen.

When the mermaid had finished reading from the document, the assembly of council representatives swam up out of their chairs, applauding, shaking hands, and shouting jubilantly.

"I don't understand," said Brynn. "What just happened?"

Her parents turned to look at her.

"It means," said Dana, "that it's not against the law to harm the humans anymore."

"It'll allow Phaedra and others to do things like sinking ships without any consequences," said Adrian.

Brynn thought about all the times she'd confronted the sea witch, and how she'd helped the police bring Phaedra to justice. She'd been on the right side, and Phaedra had been doing bad things. Now it seemed that the bad things that Phaedra had done (and the bad things she was probably planning) were not wrong. They were right. Brynn had felt afraid of the sea witch since practically the first moment they'd met, but the rules and laws of the sea had been on Brynn's side, so no matter how bad it had gotten, Brynn always knew somehow that someone would help, someone would set things right.

Now, the situation was different. Now, the law was on Phaedra's side. What if Phaedra got the government to pass a law saying it was okay for her to take revenge on Brynn?

Brynn furrowed her eyebrows. "I still don't understand. So now we *should* sink ships?"

Dana shook her head. "Brynn, sometimes the people who make the rules make mistakes. I think this is one of those mistakes."

Brynn tilted her head. "Well, if the rules can be wrong sometimes, how am I supposed to know what is right or wrong or what I should do?"

"Brynn," said Adrian, "There's the legal law, which is set by the Undersea Peace Council, but then there's another higher law, too. A moral law."

"What's that?" asked Brynn.

"The moral law is the basis for the merfolk oath. Unlike the legal law, this isn't set by anyone specifically, but it basically means we all agree we mustn't do things that hurt others. If you try to understand others and listen to your heart, you'll know if something is against the moral law," said Dana.

"But what if they are hurting us?" Brynn asked.

"The humans don't even know we exist," said Adrian. "Sinking their ships or damaging their ports won't help them to change their ways. That's more about getting revenge."

"Do you think this is the thing we were, what's the word? Anticipating?" asked Brynn. "This is the thing that we thought was going to happen?"

"Probably," said Adrian. "This is a pretty big thing, and it may require us to be very faithful to the merfolk oath."

"But what can we do?" asked Brynn. "We can't hurt the humans, but we can't allow them to ruin the oceans, right?"

Adrian frowned and Dana wrung her hands together. Brynn could tell she was making them uncomfortable.

"You know," said Dana, "sometimes we make assumptions about people because we don't know them. We don't understand them, and maybe they make us a little bit afraid."

Brynn knew Dana was talking about the humans, but for some reason Brynn was thinking all about Priscilla.

"Maybe instead of trying to hurt them back, we could try to understand them. And I am positive that if there were a lot of us working together, we could come up with a creative solution to solve this problem, without hurting others," said Dana.

Adrian nodded. "When there are a lot of people working together to make the world a better place, I don't think they can fail."

"But it's too late, isn't it?" Brynn asked. "They've already changed the law."

"So, we'll do what we can to get it changed back," said Adrian.

"We'll talk to others and set an example," said Dana.

"And no matter what, we follow the mer-oath," said Brynn. "To be a protector of the ocean and a guardian of the sea. Wherever living things need help, *including humans*, that's where we'll be!"

Adrian and Dana chuckled.

"That's right, kiddo," said Adrian. "You've got it."

CHAPTER FIFTEEN

*E*ven after school resumed, Brynn thought about what her parents had discussed with her. She especially thought a lot about the part where they said that when a large number of caring people get together, they can come up with creative solutions. That impressed Brynn. She wanted to protect the ocean, but she wanted to protect the humans, too. This was a big job, more than one little mermaid could do all on her own. She needed help.

And so Brynn wasn't thinking at all about how Jade wasn't waiting for her at the speed-current again that day. Or how Jade and Priscilla left her out when they went to practice singing. Or how Priscilla's family was so rich they could afford anything they wanted.

No. Brynn was thinking of what she could do to fulfill the merfolk oath and, surprisingly, when she stopped thinking about her friendship troubles, they almost seemed to drift away, like flotsam on the sea. And when this happened, Brynn felt excited and brave and happy because she knew what she was doing was right.

The first thing Brynn would have to do was to find others who felt the same way she did. These could be friends, fellow middle-school students, relatives, or even just people around town. She thought of all the people she knew who probably thought the same as she did—Jade, Jade's parents, Will, Will's mom, the nice lady next door, and even Windy Meyers and other teachers at Crystal Water Middle School. In fact, almost everyone Brynn knew felt the same way—that it was wrong to hurt humans, even if they did throw their garbage into the sea.

Once Brynn had banded together with other like-minded people, together they could brainstorm and make a plan to help make the ocean a better place for everyone without harm or violence. It might take time, but it could work.

And so Brynn was pretty excited when she got on the speed-current that morning. And she was positively giddy by the time she reached the school. Her head was full of ideas and positivity as she swam away from the speed-current and toward the school. The sun was beaming down and the sea was fresh and beautiful.

Brynn dove through the front doors with a huge

smile on her face—which almost instantly vanished. Inside the school, it wasn't hard to tell that even though her own attitude was positive and the day was gorgeous, something at school was very, very different.

CHAPTER SIXTEEN

*T*he first thing Brynn noticed was that everyone was wearing the Swymbits. Before it may have *seemed* like everyone else wore Symbits, but now it really was everyone. Brynn looked at the wrist of every mer-kid around every corner of every hallway. Every mermaid had one. Every merboy had one. Brynn couldn't see a single student, teacher, janitor, or lunch lady without one of the annoying little gizmos.

Even Brynn had to admit they were pretty cool-looking, and they had interesting functions, games, and apps. If Brynn had a Swymbit, she could talk to Jade anytime she wanted to. She could ask Jade why everyone was acting so weird lately. She could ask Jade lots of stuff. But Brynn didn't have one, and she still didn't want one, just on principle. Just the idea of them was annoying, and besides that, the Swymbits were a reminder of her changing friendship with Jade, and that wasn't anything she wanted to be reminded of.

Brynn swam on through the hallways of the school and noticed two things that concerned her. First, all the Swymbits winked and blinked the familiar green light that Brynn had been seeing lately. She didn't know what the green light meant because she didn't have a Swymbit herself. However, now that there were so many Swymbits to be seen—one on the wrist of every one of the hundreds of middle school students—Brynn noticed that they all blinked green *in unison*. They all blinked green on and off at the same time. This seemed important or meaningful in some way, but how? Why would they all blink at once?

The second thing that Brynn noticed was the alarming discussions she heard in the hallways and even in class. It seemed everyone was fixated on the humans and keeping them out of the ocean.

As Brynn passed by the lockers, a tall, black-haired mermaid said to her friend, "My mom says that things are going to be great once we drive all the humans away from the oceans."

In math class the teacher asked, "If each human throws 5 pounds of garbage into the ocean each day, how many pounds of garbage will 125 humans throw into the garbage in 3 weeks?"

In the hallway between classes, Brynn heard a

cross little merboy say, "All the problems we have in Fulgent are because we've been too nice to the humans!"

In science class, the teacher taught the students about the laws of motion and followed it up by saying, "If a human boat is in motion, there must be an equal and opposite force to stop it."

Everywhere Brynn went that day, she heard students and teachers alike muttering about the humans and how they were destroying the ocean.

At lunchtime, Brynn swam into the cafeteria and the chatter continued. She was relieved to see Will. Surely, he wouldn't be part of this insane idea to hurt the humans and chase them from the sea. She sat down at the table across from Will. He was rubbing his temples, the green light of his Swymbit blinking along with everyone else's.

"Hi, Will," said Brynn, nibbling at her fish sticks. "Is everything okay? You seem upset."

"Just frustrated," said Will with a long sigh.

"You, too? I knew it. Everything seems to be going a bit crazy today, doesn't it?"

"Yeah," replied Will. "And it's all because of humans and evil pollution and trash. We need to find a way to be rid of them."

"What? Why are you saying that?" Brynn asked.

"It's a big problem, Brynn," said Will. "We've got to stop them before they destroy the whole ocean."

"But what about the mer-oath?" Brynn asked.

For a moment, Will's expression softened, as though he hadn't considered the merfolk oath and its promise to protect *all* life. But he didn't answer Brynn's question, and soon his expression was sour again, and Brynn could tell he was distracted and confused.

Brynn was feeling quite confused herself, but apparently Will was not going to be of any help today. And so Brynn ate a little of her lunch, gave Will a curt, "See you around," and hurried out of the cafeteria.

At last it was time for magic class, her favorite subject. Surely, in Mrs. Meyer's class, there'd be none of this crazy talk about garbage and humans and sinking ships. Brynn swam into the classroom, and Mrs. Meyers gave her a nod and a smile. Brynn smiled back and then took her seat. Will swam in and sat in the seat behind her. Brynn could hear Will muttering to himself.

"Maybe if we got some big nets, we could capture lots of the humans at once and send them back home in big batches." He was sketching diagrams and notes in a notebook. "Maybe we could haul the nets with whales. They'd probably be glad to help—" he trailed off with a wicked chuckle.

Brynn sighed and rolled her eyes.

Mrs. Meyers swam to the front of the classroom and smiled. "Hello, class. Who's ready to learn some magic?" she asked.

Brynn sat up straight in her chair, smiled, and raised her hand.

"All right," said Mrs. Meyers. "Let's talk about how we can use magic to protect the ocean."

Finally, thought Brynn. *Some reasonable, sensible talk.*

"Let's say you're out in your favorite part of the ocean, and you see some humans," said Mrs. Meyers. "What are some ways we can use magic to force them back onto land, where they belong?"

Brynn's mouth dropped open.

Chelsea raised her hand. "A sleep spell."

"That's a good start," said Mrs. Meyers, "but then they'd sorta still be in the ocean, wouldn't they? We want them out. What are some other ideas?"

Marcus said, "If there was a group of humans, you could use sleep and stun spells on some of them, and then maybe the other humans would get scared and take the stunned and sleeping humans away."

"I like the way you're thinking, Marcus," said Mrs. Meyers.

Brynn couldn't believe her ears.

"What about some huge nets," said Will feverishly. "We could use magic to cast the nets over the humans and trap large numbers of them."

Brynn turned in her seat and looked at Will. His eyes glimmered with dark obsession. Brynn was going to say, "William Beach! What has gotten into you?" but Mrs. Meyers interrupted.

"Hmm," she said, "interesting idea, William. I'm listening."

"I was thinking we could enchant some whales to drag the nets away," Will continued. "Far away!"

"Yes, yes," said Mrs. Meyers. "Keep working on that plan, Will."

Practically every student had his or her hand up. Apparently every mer-kid in magic class had a plan to use magic to hurt, punish, and drive off the humans—including Mrs. Meyers!

"Stop it!" said Brynn, swimming out of her seat and floating above the class. "I can't take it anymore. The humans aren't our enemies! They're just like us, only they live on land. We can't stop the garbage and pollution problem by hurting them, chasing them away, or even drowning them. That's not the mer-way! We just need to work together and be creative. We can figure it out, but we should work *with* the humans and not *hurt* anyone."

Now it was her teacher and classmates who looked shocked and confused. Brynn found the entire class staring at her. She swam to Mrs. Meyers' desk and faced the class.

"Everyone, please," pleaded Brynn, "can't you see? It's just like the mer-oath says: *Wherever living beings need help, that's where I'll be.* Well, the humans are living beings, and now it's them who need our help. There are lot of angry mers and dagons and selkies and others, too. And the sea witch, of course, but if enough people join together, we can protect the humans *and* the oceans. Are you with me?"

Brynn wasn't exactly sure what she had expected her classmates to do. She had thought that maybe they'd rise out of their seats in exclamations of agreement. Or maybe they'd nod their heads in support and start working out plans.

What she didn't expect was what happened next.

"Brynn Finley!" Mrs. Meyers shouted. "Stop this right now, or you'll find yourself in the principal's office—or worse."

Brynn had never had a teacher shout at her before, especially not her favorite teacher from her favorite class.

"But Mrs. Meyers—" Brynn began to say, but Mrs. Meyers wouldn't let her finish.

"Not another word," said Mrs. Meyers. "Get your things and go see Principal Shipley in the office."

Brynn felt the eyes of the entire class on her. She thought she might cry, and she could definitely feel the red burning of her blushing cheeks. However, even in the middle of this embarrassment, she noticed the little green blinking light on Mrs. Meyers' Swymbit, and the way all the Swymbits in the room blinked along with it.

As she put her books in her bag, Will leaned over and whispered. "What's wrong with you?" he asked. "Supporting humans? Are you crazy?"

Brynn wanted to ask Will what was wrong with

him, but she knew it wouldn't do any good—Will had a strange look on his face. It was like he wasn't himself but someone who was imitating William Beach. She looked at him for a moment, but then hitched her backpack onto her back. Mrs. Meyers was at her desk with her hands on her hips, waiting for Brynn to leave the room.

Brynn hung her head and swam toward the door. Soon she was sitting in a chair across from Mr. Shipley in his office. She didn't want to be in trouble, but Brynn thought maybe she'd finally be able to get some answers about what was going on.

"Ms. Finley," said Mr. Shipley in a grave tone, "we don't usually have any issues with you, do we?"

"Well," mumbled Brynn sheepishly, "not lately."

"Good point," said Mr. Shipley. "Listen, Ms. Finley. Don't you want to be a good student?"

"Yes, sir," said Brynn. "I very much do."

"Well, don't you like your magic class?"

"I do, sir, it's my favorite class," said Brynn.

Mr. Shipley adjusted his glasses. "I don't understand, then. What was the reason for this outburst?"

"Mr. Shipley!" cried Brynn, "The whole class was talking about casting spells on humans and sinking ships and hurting people!"

Mr. Shipley nodded his head and said, "Mm. Yes, go on."

Finally, thought Brynn, *someone who will listen to reason.*

"Even Mrs. Meyers was talking about it—she was collecting ideas from us about how to kick all the humans out of the ocean!"

"Yes, yes," said Mr. Shipley. "Tell me the problem."

"Well, that's it. It goes against the mer-oath to protect living things."

Mr. Shipley clucked his tongue reprovingly. "I'm afraid you're not seeing this the right way, Ms. Finley. Haven't you seen all the destruction the humans have caused? Why, there's a section of coral reef right here in Fulgent that is almost completely dead. I saw it myself."

"Yes, I saw it too, sir."

"Do you think that it is okay to destroy the reefs? I have to tell you, Brynn, you must not know how important reefs are to the ocean if you think that is okay."

"No, I don't think it's okay. But two wrongs don't make a right, Principal Shipley."

Principal Shipley folded his arms against his broad mid-section and Brynn could see his Swymbit flashing green. Just like everyone else's.

"I understand now," said Principal Shipley.

Brynn sat up straight. "Oh, you do? I'm so glad, because I was beginning to feel that I'm the only one who—"

"Yes, I understand that you are a trouble-maker."

"Wha—?"

"We will not tolerate such behavior at Crystal Water Middle School. I'm assigning you to detention and this will go on your permanent record. And I better not hear about you causing any more trouble or you'll be facing expulsion!"

"But I'm just trying to follow the merfolk oath!" cried Brynn. "This isn't fair!"

"Fair? Fair! You talk to me about fair? Tell me, Ms. Finley. How is it fair that the humans can contaminate the places where we live and face no consequences? How is it fair that our waters are polluted? That our livelihoods are affected by the land-dwellers? What is fair is to hold them accountable for their actions—to make them pay!"

"But—" Brynn said.

"Leave my office now, Ms. Finley. Go home before you get yourself into more trouble."

Brynn grabbed her things and sulked out of the office. Was there no one else who felt the way she did?

Her parents!

She knew they would never want harm to come to the humans. Brynn wanted to go home as soon as possible.

CHAPTER SEVENTEEN

*B*rynn raced away to the speed-current stop near the school, and hopped on the current to get home. She was soon out of breath, but she swam on quickly. When she got to her house, she threw open the door and dove inside.

"Mom! Dad!" she cried.

She may or may not have closed the door—she was too excited to think about that. And her entrance was so abrupt and noisy, she frightened Tully, who was napping on the couch in the living room. He darted under the couch, then stuck his nose out cautiously.

"Sorry, Tully!" said Brynn. She began whirling through the house. "Mom! Dad! Are you home?"

She found both of them in the kitchen.

They looked at her as though she was a ghost.

"Sweetie?" asked Brynn's mom. "What are you doing here?"

Her dad said, "Yeah, why aren't you at school?"

Brynn huffed and sighed. "Oh my oceans! I've had the worst day! I'm so upset! Just wait until you hear what was going on at school! Everyone's wearing Swymbits, and they're all blinking green, and even Mrs. Meyers is against the humans now, and at first I thought Mr. Shipley was on my side, but then he wasn't and so he said, 'Get out of my office!' and so then I got on the speed-current and—"

"Whoa, whoa, whoa," said Adrian holding up his hands. He chuckled sympathetically. "I only got about half of that."

Dana said, "Yeah, dear. Back up, start again, slow down, and tell us what's going on."

Brynn shared everything that she'd seen and heard and said that day—all the mutterings about the humans, the plans to defeat them, the weirdly blinking Swymbits, and how bizarre it was that even Will and Mrs. Meyers agreed. She ended with magic class and being sent to the principal's office.

"I don't know, Brynn," said Dana. "The humans *have* caused a lot of damage to the ocean. Maybe it is time that we took action."

"What?" cried Brynn. "That's not what you said last night! You both said they were living beings, and so we shouldn't hurt them."

"We can only take so much," said Adrian with a

sad shrug of his shoulders. "I think the others are right. We should probably listen to them."

Now Brynn felt so confused that she wasn't sure she could even speak anymore. Who was next? Tully? Would he want to start chasing humans off the ocean and away from the beaches? Brynn's parents had always taught her to listen to her heart in order to know what was right or wrong. Her heart was telling her very clearly that, even though humans were causing serious damage to the oceans, it was wrong for merfolk to hurt humans!

"In fact," added Dana, "some mers are conducting a search party tonight to find humans in the area so that we can begin to hold them accountable. Your father and I have been discussing this, and we think you should join us. You've been helping out with mer-magic missions to assist sea-life, and we think you could help us out with rounding up some of these polluting humans."

"Accountable? What does that mean? You mean let them have a trial with the Undersea Peace Council?" asked Brynn.

"No, no," said Adrian, shaking his head. "It seems like we're past the point of trials," said Adrian. "We have to take matters into our own hands now. We have to solve these problems ourselves."

"Yes," cried Brynn. "We need to solve these problems with teamwork, creativity, and kindness. Just like we were talking about *yesterday!*"

"Think of it this way, Brynn," said Adrian. "There wouldn't be a problem if there *were no humans*."

Brynn felt a chill climb up her tail and back.

"What's wrong with you guys? What's wrong with everyone? Why is everyone acting so strange?" asked Brynn.

"Maybe we've just gained some—clarity over the subject," said Dana.

She brushed Brynn's hair away from Brynn's eyes, with a caring gesture, and as she did, Brynn noticed the new Swymbit on her mother's wrist, with that same eerie green light, flashing steadily.

Brynn's eyes darted immediately in her dad's direction. He was holding his chin in his hand, and there on his wrist was Swymbit.

"Wait, you guys got *Swymbits*?" Brynn asked. "When did this happen?"

"Oh, yes," said Dana, her eyes brightening with a feverish light. "We nearly forgot to tell you! Aren't they neat? We got one for you, too."

Brynn watched in horror as her mother produced the familiar Swymbit box. She slid it open and took out a Swymbit.

It was beautiful. The Swymbit was coral-colored and the wristband shimmered with sea jewels and mother-of-pearl. And in the box, there were other pretty wristbands to choose from.

Brynn's eyes widened. The Swymbit seemed to draw her slowly closer. She thought of all the fun she could have with it—playing games, sharing videos with Jade, listening to music. It was beginning to seem like she was the only person in all of Fulgent who didn't have one, so why shouldn't she finally give in and wear one like everyone else?

"Give me your wrist," said Dana.

But there was something odd about her mother's voice.

"No!" said Brynn. She backed away from the sparkly little gizmo. "I don't want it!"

"Why not?" said Adrian, reaching out for Brynn. "Don'tcha like it? They're really useful, and a lotta fun. Just try it on. See if ya like it."

"No!" yelled Brynn, and she tried to swim away but her parents had her.

"Let me just put it on you," said Dana. There was something robotic about her voice. "Then we'll show you how to use it, and then maybe we can talk some more about the humans and how to solve these various problems."

There was something wrong with her parents. It wasn't like them to act this way. Not at all!

Just then, Tully swam into the kitchen. He was quivering with excitement, as though he figured they were all playing together, and he wanted to join in. He circled them a few times and then shoved and nosed his way between them. As he did so, he bumped Dana's arm, and the new Swymbit flew out of her hand. Dana and Adrian let go of Brynn and fumbled around to grab the Swymbit, which was tumbling down through the water.

"Let's get out of here!" Brynn yelled, and she and Tully swam for the door. As soon as they got outside, Brynn grabbed Tully, zapped him with a speed spell, and cried, "To the kelp forest!"

Brynn considered the possibility that Tully had actually figured out what had been going on there in the kitchen. Or maybe he didn't know exactly what was going on, but sensed danger. It was hard to tell with Tully—he always had kind of a sleepy, half-smile on his face, even when he was afraid or worried.

Brynn would never know if he'd helped her on purpose or by chance, but "To the kelp forest!" was all he needed to hear. He zoomed out of town, pulling Brynn behind him and leaving a trail of tiny, nervous bubbles in their wake.

Soon Brynn and Tully were safe in the confines of the swaying strands of dark-green kelp. The long, ribbon-like leaves spiraled and twisted in the slow current, and the sunlight filtered down in warm, glittering beams.

The peaceful kelp forest usually had a calming effect on Brynn, and today was no exception. There was still a lot to think about, and there were plans to make. Still, Brynn took a deep breath, looked around at her beloved forest, and thought for a long while.

"Tully," she finally said, "Something really

strange is going on. I *know* my parents, and they've never acted this way before. Same with Will and Mrs. Meyers. I would never expect anyone I know to say the things I heard today. Revenge on the humans? Driving them away from the ocean? Punishing them? Hurting and drowning them? It's cruel! Barbaric! It's like they all get those silly Swymbits and then they lost their minds!"

Tully looked at Brynn and blinked his big, sleepy eyes a few times.

And then Brynn had a thought. Not just a thought —an idea. And not just an idea—the solution!

She snapped her fingers. "That's it! I know what's going on. The Swymbits are controlling them!"

Tully tilted his head curiously.

"It sounds crazy, but it's the only solution. Everyone who has been talking about getting revenge on the humans and punishing them has a Swymbit. Mom and Dad were talking about peace, love, and understanding yesterday, but now that they have Swymbits, they've changed their minds completely. Will got a Swymbit, and now he's saying things I've never heard him say. And there's that weird blinking green light—they're all in unison! It all fits together now!"

Tully's eyes widened, as though he might almost understand.

Brynn thought for another few moments and said, "But it's not just the Swymbits. The Swymbits are just watches that have games, music, videos, and really super cute little interchangeable wristbands. The Swymbits aren't controlling everyone; someone is using the Swymbits to control everyone. And I think I'm pretty sure I know who!"

Tully looked as though he were trying figure out who, too, but before he had much time to think about it, Brynn zapped him with another speed spell and said, "Take us back to town, boy!"

And that was all he needed to hear.

CHAPTER EIGHTEEN

*T*ully cruised along like a barracuda, swerving through the kelp forest, dashing over the sea urchins spread across the sandy sea floor, and out into the open water on the way to Fulgent.

Brynn held onto Tully's shell. Tully seemed to hardly notice her.

They sped through a school of dream fish, scattering them in every direction. They startled an octopus, who squirted a cloud of dark ink as it fled away. Soon Fulgent came into view, which was good because Brynn was getting tired from holding onto Tully's shell at such velocity.

For his part, Tully seemed to be having the time of his life. His grin was even wider than usual. Although sea turtles were strong, able to swim long distances, and stay underwater for great lengths of time, they usually didn't get to swim at such high speeds. Tully was hauling along like he could swim clear around the globe before nightfall.

It might have been easier if Brynn had taken the speed-current back to town, but then she'd have to leave Tully behind, and Brynn didn't want to do that. Even though he was just her pet sea turtle, he was, frankly, the only one of Brynn's acquaintances who was acting normally at the moment.

Brynn had decided that she needed to go get help, just like she and Will had gotten help when the sea witch was trying to destroy the cruise ship. However, it was a little different this time. Who could help her if everyone was being controlled through their Swymbits? Brynn knew she had to act fast before the entire town of Fulgent, or even all the mers in the ocean, were taken over by these silly and trendy little sea-lectronic devices.

When Tully and Brynn reached town, Brynn said, "Tully. You're the best sea turtle in the whole wide ocean, but I need you to go home now."

Tully looked worried.

"Don't worry. I'm going to go get help. This will all be over soon."

Tully gave a little nod of the head and turned back in the direction of their home. The speed spell was still on him, and he swam away as quick as a herring. Brynn knew he'd probably take twenty laps around the house before settling down, but she thought that'd be all right.

Now Brynn zapped herself with a speed spell, which she used to swim to the middle of town very quickly. The police had been watching the area closely both because of the Undersea Peace Council meeting and because of the sea witch's trial. Officer McScales had told Brynn personally that if she ever needed help, all she had to do was ask. And did she need help now?

Oh, boy, do I.

She reached the courthouse and was relieved to see the strong figure of Officer McScales patrolling around the courthouse.

"Officer McScales! Officer McScales!" Brynn cried. "I need help!"

Officer McScales turned toward Brynn, a look of recognition on his face as he swam rapidly toward her.

"Why, Brynn Finley," he said. "I'm happy to help. What's wrong?"

"The Swymbits, sir," said Brynn. "First, at school, everyone was talking about the humans and even Mrs. Meyers who teaches magic and is my favorite teacher and usually really, really kind and smart, and just like I want to be when I grow up, well, even *she* was behaving oddly, and then I got in trouble with the principal, but I shouldn't have because I was just trying to protect the humans, and even my *mom and dad* were wearing Swymbits, and have you noticed how they all blink green at the same time, and so they tried to put a Swymbit on me, but my turtle, Tully, jumped in and saved me and, and—" Brynn paused to take a deep breath. "—I think the Swymbits are controlling people's minds! We need to get them off of everyone!"

It was at precisely that moment that Brynn happened to glance at Officer McScale's wrist, of course, and she realized that he was also wearing a flashing green Swymbit.

Brynn gasped.

Officer McScales motioned to some other merfolk and dagons that were in the area and began swimming closer to Brynn.

"I think you may be mistaken, Ms. Finley. I don't think the Swymbits are the trouble at all," said Officer McScales with a wicked grin. "They're actually really nifty, with fitness goals, videos, and games."

"I was afraid you might say that," said Brynn.

"Ah, don't be afraid. See, I've come around to thinking the sea witch was right, and we all should have been listening to her. I think you'll agree with us soon."

Brynn gulped. "I was afraid you were going to say that, too."

"I also happen to know the sea witch is looking for you right now," said Officer McScales. "I think maybe we should pay her a visit." From his belt he unclipped a pair of magical handcuffs.

Phaedra! Brynn just knew it had to be her. How had she done it? How had she figured out how to control everyone though the Swymbits?

By this point, Officer McScales was right in front of Brynn, and the others he had motioned to were surrounding her. Brynn's hands were shaking.

"I haven't done anything wrong," said Brynn.

"You're a human-lover," spat a dagon.

"The mer-oath says—" Brynn began, but she was cut off by Officer McScales and the shouting of just about everyone around them.

"Ah, we all know what the oath says!" they cried angrily. "You don't have to tell us!"

Brynn wasn't sure what this crowd intended to do with her, but she did know that they all looked very angry, and yet they had that odd, robotic look on their faces—everyone who wore a Swymbit wore the same expression. It was obvious that they weren't thinking for themselves. How could Brynn find anyone to help her when everyone was being controlled by the sea witch?

Brynn closed her eyes and put her hands together, trying to conjure a bubble of protection around herself. It was a spell she had never had much success with, but she thought in this moment of desperation she might make it work.

Officer McScales swam in her direction.

Brynn's sphere of magic grew between her hands. It was working!

Officer McScales floated closer, a stern frown on his face.

The sphere began to engulf Brynn, just as it was supposed to. She'd done it!

Officer McScales reached out to take her by the arm.

Brynn's protection bubble popped and made a fizzling sound.

I've really got to get a tutor to learn that spell, thought Brynn.

But she'd had a lot of success that day with the speed spell, so she quickly conjured that. Perhaps she could speed away back to the kelp forest or at least evade capture until she could figure out what to do next.

But it was too late. As soon as she put her hands together to begin the magic, Officer McScales clapped the magical handcuffs onto her wrists. These not only chained her wrists together like any other handcuffs would, the mer-police cuffs were enchanted with powerful mer-magic that kept the wearer from using magic to escape. Brynn was good and truly captured.

"Oh, no you don't," said Officer McScales. "We're taking you to see Phaedra."

CHAPTER NINETEEN

*P*lease let this be a nightmare.

Please let this be a nightmare.

Ordinarily, Brynn hated having bad dreams, just like anyone else. However, now she thought she'd give almost anything to know that everything happening to her was a bad dream. It would definitely be one of the better nightmares she'd had in her life—it had dire consequences and chase scenes, narrow escapes, mind control, and angry mobs, and it even had the sea witch as a main character. Brynn pressed her eyes together hoping beyond hope that she would wake up and it would all go away.

But she didn't wake up, and she knew it was too real. The whole ocean had turned on its head.

Officer McScales and a few other angry seafolk were now escorting Brynn to see Phaedra. The mind-controlled police officer had placed magical handcuffs on Brynn, but she probably wouldn't have been able to escape, anyway. She'd seen Officer McScales and the other Fulgent police in action, and she knew they were fast, strong, and very good at mer-magic.

Brynn also knew that they wouldn't act this way if not for the sea witch's wicked plans. She tried not to blame McScales and the others as they pushed her forward through the ocean. Soon, Phaedra the sea witch would finally carry out revenge for all the times Brynn had foiled her schemes and plots.

Brynn could barely believe that, just a week earlier, her biggest problem had been some jealous little spats with her best friend. And she'd been making plans with her dad to see Jay Barracuda and the Killer Whales in concert. She'd been hanging out with Will and talking about outfits and setlists and souvenir t-shirts.

Her troubles with Jade and Priscilla seemed so insignificant compared to being taken to the sea witch, who was at that moment probably conjuring the spell that would finally turn Brynn into a squishy, insignificant sea slug.

Brynn whimpered a little, but Officer McScales prodded her along.

"Keep on swimmin'," he said. "Don't try anything."

After swimming for what seemed like miles (Brynn thought it would have been very considerate of Officer McScales to use a speed spell), they reached a deep and gloomy-looking area of the ocean at the edges the Craggy Deep. Here there was no coral or kelp or colorful urchins marching along the sea floor. Here there was only dull gray rock and the occasional slithering of sea worms and hagfish. Dark and gloomy sediment hung in the water.

Brynn spotted Ian Fletcher the dagon. When he saw Brynn and Officer McScales, his face broke into a fishy grin, and he paddled eagerly over to them. His long claws sliced through the water as he swam around Brynn, looking at her like a captured morsel that he might eat for supper.

"My, my, my," he purred. His smile revealed row upon row of sharp little teeth. "Well, well, well. It's my little mermaid friend. How I've missed you! Oh, and Phaedra has, too. She will be simply delighted to see you again!"

Brynn refused to say anything to him. She was scared out of her mind, but she managed to spitefully scowl at Ian Fletcher.

"You are all in luck," said Ian. "Phaedra should be here any minute. Well done, Officer McScales."

Officer McScales nodded. "My pleasure," he said, and his Swymbit's green light seemed to flash more brightly than before.

A police officer and Ian Fletcher getting along? Even working together? thought Brynn with rising panic. The sea really was turned completely upside down!

Then the water began rushing past them and

swirling around them. The sediment cleared away, and a small, purple point of light appeared among them. It burned more and more brightly as they watched. It grew in size. The water swirled. Brynn squinted against the brightness, and just when she thought she could withstand it no more, the light burst with a thunderclap into a dazzling shower of black and purple sparks.

And there she was—Phaedra!—floating tall and magnificent in her magical power and glory. Her hands were outstretched, palms up. Her long, silky hair spread around her like a headdress in the water.

Brynn's teeth clattered with fright, but even she admitted to herself once again that Phaedra was as beautiful as she was terrifying.

Phaedra's eyes roved over Brynn, her wrists in handcuffs and Officer McScales and Ian Fletcher to either side. She smiled.

"Hello, everyone," Phaedra drawled. "What a lovely greeting party."

Ian bowed deeply at the sight of Phaedra. When Officer McScales and the others saw this, they bowed as well. But Brynn, in an act of defiance, despite her fear, only lifted her chin higher.

"I'm so very glad you all could make time to meet with me today," said Phaedra. "You, especially, Brynn Finley."

There was something in Phaedra's tone that broke

Brynn's courage momentarily. She gulped audibly and shrank down between McScales and Ian.

Phaedra rose a little higher in the water, until she was looking down on Brynn and the others. The water was still swirling slightly. The gray gloomy sediment created a sort of dark curtain around them. Phaedra floated above them, her beautiful lips parted in a soft smile.

"Tonight," she said. "Tonight we take back the ocean from those who would harm her. Tonight we send a message to the humans by destroying every boat and pier we can. Tonight we take our revenge!"

Everyone but Brynn raised their arms and cheered.

Phaedra stopped and stared at Brynn, and then she descended from her place high in the water.

"Why, Brynn Finley, won't you join us?" cooed Phaedra. "Don't you wish to protect the ocean? You do follow the mer-oath, don't you?" She was floating down through the water and she came to a stop when she was face to face with Brynn.

Brynn tried to turn away. She shook her head. Her parents had taught Brynn the mer-oath when she was just a little mer-toddler, and after seeing her parents help whales and sharks and turtles and sardines, and after seeing them make the ocean a better place with peace, love, and understanding, Brynn knew it was a wicked thing for Phaedra to use the mer-oath to justify hurting people and getting revenge.

"Why not, little one? I thought *you* of all people would want to be a guardian of the sea. You have so much mer-magical potential. You could be of such great help to me—if only you would stop this ridiculous meddling and resisting and questioning and *thinking for yourself!*"

And with that, Phaedra conjured a blinding explosion of magical energy to punctuate her wrath. Everyone, including Officer McScales, drew back from Phaedra, shielding their faces with their arms and hands. Water rushed over them all, sending their hair and beards flailing in the water. The dark sediment was pushed back, but it pressed in upon them oppressively again, and the darkness deepened.

"There are *people* on those boats and piers and docks," said Brynn. She was so afraid now that her voice was barely a squeak, but she felt she had to keep speaking up. "*Living beings.* Just like it says in the mer-oath."

"You disappoint me, Brynn," muttered Phaedra. "Such—great—potential. I saw it from the very first time we met. You remember that I mentioned it, don't you, Brynn?"

Brynn nodded.

"Strong magic," said Phaedra. "Powerful magic. And smart, too, obviously. I could teach you so much."

Mer-magic came from love. Brynn knew the sea witch's power was fueled by other things—like anger and jealousy and a want for revenge. Even if Phaedra's magic *was* more powerful, Brynn didn't want to have anything to do with it.

"I'm not interested," squeaked Brynn, trying to keep her expression plain so she wouldn't reveal how afraid she really felt.

"A pity," said Phaedra. "So you won't help in the fight against the humans? You know, I think even your friends and family are on board with my plan. But not you?"

Brynn shook her head.

"Then what shall I do with you? Ah, I know!" Phaedra pushed back the sleeves of her black flowing dress and raised her hands.

This was it. This was the moment Brynn became a lowly sea slug. She cowered, covered her face with her hands, and cried, "Please don't turn me into a sea slug!"

Phaedra paused and said, "Please don't what?"

"Please don't turn me into a sea slug." Brynn kept her hands over her face, just in case.

"A sea slug? Why in the ocean would I turn anyone into a sea slug?"

"You weren't going to?"

Phaedra was plainly astonished that Brynn had thought such a thing. She laughed. "No, of course not!"

"Do you mind me asking what you *were* going to do?" squeaked Brynn.

"Well, I hadn't really made up my mind," said Phaedra offhandedly. "I like to play it by ear when I obliterate someone. It's more creative that way, more impressive. It'd never occurred to me to turn you into a sea slug. What put that idea in your head?"

"Just a rumor, I guess," said Brynn, face still buried in her hands. "Something I heard at school."

Phaedra laughed. "Such prestidigitation is far beneath me."

Brynn felt a slight measure of relief, and then nothing happened for several moments. Brynn dared to peek out between her fingers.

Phaedra was tapping her chin, a sort of clever smile spreading over her lovely, pale face. "Although," she said, "now that you mention it, it *is* a very interesting idea. Getting rid of the humans will be a lot of work. If we sink their ships, drive them off the beaches, and even drown them, more will just return. They're always making more boats, more docks, and more sea-side resorts."

Officer McScales and the others appeared to be hanging on Phaedra's every word.

"But if, as Brynn Finley suggests, I turn them all into sea slugs, we wouldn't have to drive them away or sink their boats. No, they'd just stay here with us, where they could be put to very good use—eating debris, clearing the seafloor of detritus and litter."

Brynn groaned. Phaedra turned her attention to the others.

"Officer McScales, do you think the merfolk magic could help with this?"

"I think we probably could, ma'am. We're not in the habit of turning anyone or anything into sea slugs, but we could probably figure it out if you were to teach us."

"Excellent! Gather everyone up then and have them meet here at dusk. I'll teach the spell—it really won't be too complicated—and then we'll rid the world of humans! They'll be so much cuter as sea slugs."

Phaedra began swimming, or rather floating away, but Ian called out to her. "Phaedra, aren't you forgetting something?"

"Hmm, what?" asked Phaedra.

"This little mermaid," Ian said, motioning with his head toward Brynn.

"Ah, yes," said Phaedra. "How could I forget?"

Brynn covered her face again. *Here comes the spell,* she thought. She bit her bottom lip, hoping that whatever it was it wouldn't be too painful and would be over quick.

"I think I'll hold off on obliterating her," announced Phaedra. "She may be of some use yet, and besides, I want her to see her idea in action. Take of those handcuffs and have her put on this, then I think you'll find she'll become most agreeable."

From the sleeve of her dress Phaedra pulled out another Swymbit, flashing green. And Brynn noticed again that Phaedra was wearing a Swymbit of her own, though hers was flashing red.

Officer McScales removed the handcuffs.

"All righty," he said to Brynn. "Now put this on." He held the Swymbit out to her.

"No," said Brynn.

"Put it on," he repeated, "or I'll have to put it on you."

"Okay, okay," said Brynn. She took the Swymbit from Officer McScales and began fumbling with it to get it fastened, but she could only use one hand, because of course she was trying to put it on her other wrist. She tried it on one wrist, then the other.

"How's this stupid thing work?" she muttered, trying awkwardly to buckle the band one-handedly.

"You have to put the one end of the band through the buckle," stammered McScales pointing and pantomiming. "No, that's backward. Turn it around and—no, just, here, let me—"

"I've got it, I've got it," assured Brynn, batting McScales away.

But Brynn was faking it all along, using the confusion to quickly conjure up a spell.

"Help her," said Phaedra wearily.

"She's got it on upside down," snapped Ian Fletcher.

"I know what I'm doing," muttered Brynn.

And she really did.

In the wink of an eye, she'd zapped up William Beach's special push spell, and she used the magic to launch the little Swymbit several hundred leagues across the ocean in the direction of the Craggy Deep. It zipped away into the dark water and disappeared into the murky sediment mist.

Phaedra let out a groan and put her face into her hand.

CHAPTER TWENTY

"*Y*ou're becoming a real pain in the tail," said Officer McScales, wagging a finger at Brynn. "You know that?"

"Well, I'm not gonna argue with you," said Brynn folding her arms with sassy satisfaction.

McScales grabbed onto Brynn's arm and turned to the sea witch. "Miss Phaedra," he said sheepishly. "Would you happen to have another Swymbit?"

"Of course I do not!" hissed Phaedra. "If I did, that would mean that I assumed a mermaid in middle-grade would outsmart Fulgent's finest police officer!"

Officer McScales's face reddened with embarrassment.

"And that," Phaedra continued, "would be a very foolish thing to assume, wouldn't it?"

McScales nodded and hung his head.

"Go and find that confounded gadget and put it on her wrist!" cried Phaedra jabbing a finger into the soupy seawater. She had lifted herself to her full and impressive height, and the swirling water around her glowed purple with her wicked rage.

McScales began to swim in the direction the Swymbit had gone, dragging Brynn along with him.

"Leave her here, you dunce!" Phaedra shouted, her voice cracking with frustration.

"But, but, she'll get away," said Officer McScales.

"Go and fetch the gadget, you clam brain!" Phaedra screamed. "I'll take care of her!"

McScales did as he was told. Phaedra reared back and lifted her arms. Brynn could see that she was already cooking up a hold spell, one so heavy and strong it would probably sting like crazy. Brynn scrunched herself down and braced for the impact of Phaedra's spell. And she didn't have to wait long— within a half second, she felt a tremendous impact.

But it didn't hurt.

In fact, it felt like she'd just been struck by a giant plastic beach ball, and immediately she felt herself being propelled through the water at a terrific velocity.

Brynn opened her eyes.

Now, of all the merfolk Brynn knew, the one she least expected to see was Priscilla Banks.

And yet, there was Priscilla.

She was covered with a very strongly reinforced

protection bubble and she was zooming Brynn through the ocean with the benefit of a speed spell!

"Hold on!" yelled Priscilla.

Brynn did her best, but it wasn't easy. Priscilla's protection bubble was big and tough, very much in fact like a giant beach ball. Brynn tried gripping it, but it was round and bouncy and terrifically difficult to get hold of it, but Brynn managed somehow not to fall off or get swept away, and she watched with astonishment as Phaedra and McScales and the rest of them receded into the far distance. They seemed to be so astonished and off-guard, they didn't know how to react.

"Wowee!" cried Brynn.

Priscilla kept up her speed spell until she and Brynn reached the edge of the Craggy Deep. Then Priscilla angled downward into the blackness of the deep, mostly likely because it seemed like a good place to hide. The darkness of the massive trench began to swallow them.

"No!" yelped Brynn. "We can't go down there! It's too dangerous!"

"Where can we go?" said Priscilla. "Remember, I'm new here!"

Priscilla angled up from the blank blackness of the Craggy Deep. Brynn looked behind them. She saw no one in pursuit.

Priscilla's got some awesome magic! Brynn thought.

The water rushed past them as they sped along.

Phaedra and the others would of course come looking for them and would use speed spells of their own, but they'd gotten a very nice head start, and it would be hard to follow anyone in such a dark and murky part of the ocean.

"Head for Mammoth Cave!" said Brynn, now in a loud whisper. "We'll hide there until we figure out what to do next."

With that, Brynn cast another speed spell and the beautiful hair of both mermaids swept back marvelously in the water as they zoomed in the direction of the cave.

When they arrived, Brynn placed a finger over her lips and signaled for Priscilla to stay quiet. Then she motioned for Priscilla to follow her to a series of hidden alcoves among the rocks that were often used by performers as dressing rooms.

"We should be very quiet," whispered Brynn, "because of the acoustics and all the echoes."

Priscilla nodded. Even Brynn's faint whisper echoed amazingly.

"Thank you for saving me from Phaedra," Brynn continued. "Thank you so much. But how'd you know I needed help? And how'd you find me?"

"I saw you by the courthouse," said Priscilla. "And I got a funny feeling that something was wrong. I was worried. So, I followed you"

"Let me guess," Brynn went on. "You used your singing to amplify your spells?"

Priscilla smiled and nodded.

"You have the most beautiful voice," said Brynn.

"Thanks," said Priscilla.

Brynn looked for a moment at Priscilla. She still had her fancy makeup and lavishly styled hair and expensive clothing, but maybe for the first time Brynn saw that she was just another mermaid, like herself.

"That was really nice of you," said Brynn. "Thanks again."

"Don't worry about it," said Priscilla.

Then Brynn looked at Priscilla's wrist, and she was relieved to see that there wasn't a Swymbit on it.

"Where's your Swymbit?" Brynn asked, pointing.

"Psh," scoffed Priscilla with a toss of her head. "That old thing? I'm over Swymbits. I mean I know my own dad, like, invented them and everything, but it seems like *everyone's* wearing them now. I never did think they were very cool—always beeping and nagging you about how far you've swum every day, and everyone always texting you and tagging you. It got to be really annoying."

Brynn nodded. "Yeah, I get it. Have you also noticed that people with Swymbits are acting weird? Like maybe the Swymbits are—"

"Controlling them? Yeah! I've wondered about that," said Priscilla. "That's not the way my father designed them. They're not supposed to work like that."

"No, I didn't think so, but I noticed Phaedra was wearing one," whispered Brynn, "and hers looked different. It had a red flashing light instead of a green one."

"She probably used her magic to hack into the Swymbit system," said Priscilla, eyes wide. "She's using the Swymbit network somehow."

"I know she can control people with her magic," said Brynn, "but not even the sea witch could cast enough control spells to control everyone at once. So, maybe with the Swymbit network, she can use one control spell to control anyone who's wearing a Swymbit."

"Whoa, that's a really evil plan," said Priscilla, shaking her head. "If it wasn't so mean, I'd almost think it was *cool*."

"Oh, she's mean all right," said Brynn. "Trust me. I know."

"I must have taken off my Swymbit before Phaedra hacked into the system to control everyone," said Priscilla.

"Wowee," said Brynn. "Everyone jumps on a trend and then, bang, they are all thinking exactly the same."

Priscilla gave her a look. "Even without the mind control, everyone dressing and acting the same way is pretty silly." She pushed at some pebbles in the sand with her tail.

Brynn rubbed her face. "Do you know anyone else who *isn't* wearing the Swymbits?"

Priscilla thought about this for a moment or two. "No," she said, "I don't. My parents both wear them, and so does all of our staff. All the teachers at school have Swymbits. Of course Jade was wearing hers last time I saw her—and she was acting weird, too."

"What do you mean?" asked Brynn. "Weird how?"

"She was just completely obsessed with humans —their pollution, their boats, how we could stop them. She wouldn't talk about anything else, so I was like, 'I'm outta here'."

"What did you do then?" Brynn asked.

"Oh, I was just heading home and I saw you at the courthouse, like I said. And I could tell something wasn't right, but I could also tell that you weren't acting bizarre."

Brynn blushed. "It's only because I'm not wearing a Swymbit."

"Yeah, but you made that choice. Even when everyone else chose to wear one, you decided to be an individual and do your own thing. I always liked that about you. I know sooo many people who just do whatever I do, and say whatever I say—because they think I'm cool or something. It was actually a nice change to meet someone who didn't copy me just because my family owns a sea-copter or something."

Brynn didn't bother to admit that the reason she didn't want a Swymbit was because she didn't really like Priscilla at first. She knew what Priscilla was talking about, and now that Brynn had gotten a chance to talk to Priscilla without all the jealousy and friend-drama, she thought Priscilla might make a pretty good friend. She didn't seem that different from any other mermaid. In fact, she was very nice. Sure, her family had a butler and a sea-copter, but that hadn't stopped her from helping Brynn.

Wowee, thought Brynn. *I would be just another one of the thousands of mindless merfolk under the control of the sea witch right now, if it hadn't been for Priscilla.*

Hidden inside the little sea crag within Mammoth Cave, Brynn began swimming back and forth the way she always did when she was deep in thought. Priscilla watched her go one way and then the other.

"Somehow," Brynn said to Priscilla, "we've got to get everyone back to normal, and we need to do it before tonight so that none of the humans will be harmed."

"Yeah," said Priscilla. "But how can we possibly get everyone to take off their Swymbits before Phaedra starts turning everyone into sea slugs?" asked Priscilla. "We need more help."

"You're right. There's no way we could even begin to take off all the Swymbits. Your dad's done a great job making Swymbits the biggest fad ever in Fulgent."

"He has a degree in sales and marketing," said Priscilla, shaking her head.

"What if we didn't have to take every Swymbit from every wrist?" said Brynn. "What if there was a different way?"

"You've got a plan?" Priscilla asked.

"I've got the concept of an idea for a plan," said Brynn.

Priscilla raised one eyebrow and said, "Well, that's a start."

"But you're right," said Brynn. "We're going to need more help."

CHAPTER TWENTY-ONE

*A*s soon as the two mermaids had returned to Fulgent, a mermaid pushing a baby stroller had pointed at them and yelled, "There's the two mermaids without Swymbits!"

Even the mer-baby in the stroller had pointed his chubby finger at them, revealing a Swymbit on his little mer-baby arm.

And that had begun the first of several times that the two mermaids were chased by other merfolk through the town of Fulgent—all of them holding up brand-new Swymbits to slap on the mermaids' wrists if they ever got close enough.

But they never did.

Brynn and Priscilla had only been able to avoid capture by using speed spells amplified by friendship and songs sang with Priscilla's crystal-clear voice and perfect pitch. Brynn was surprised they had been able to use the friendship amplifier so soon. She certainly hadn't viewed Priscilla as a friend before, but it was amazing how quickly things could change when you began thinking nicely about someone else. Brynn would later reflect that the two had become friends the moment Priscilla had bounced Brynn with Priscilla's big bubble of protection.

And so the two mermaids dashed from one part of Fulgent to another, ducking and hiding, but they knew they couldn't leave.

Not until they had found Will and Jade.

It's not as easy as you might think to find your friends when their minds are under the control of a sea witch. It's even harder when every person you encounter has been told to look for you and apprehend you. And it's hardest of all when you know that if they catch you, they'll slap a Swymbit on your wrist and your thoughts will no longer be your own.

"I wish we knew the spell for invisibility," said Brynn.

"Oh come on, that's something that isn't even taught until college," said Priscilla. "We can do this. Just think of it as a giant hide-and-seek game."

Brynn laughed. She couldn't help herself. It really was kind of a big game of hide-and-seek.

Priscilla is pretty fun. Maybe I should have given her a chance before thinking she was mean and snobbish, thought Brynn.

First, they checked at Jade's and Will's houses.

Sea caves generally didn't have lots of windows, so the two mermaids had no choice but to knock on the doors.

"We'll just knock and then hide," said Priscilla. "That way we can see if they're home."

"But what if someone else answers the door? Like their parents?"

"Hmm," said Priscilla. "Oh, I know! I'll leave something of mine behind at each house. Since everyone is on the look-out for us, they'll all come out and search."

So, at the home of Jade, Priscilla had left her beautiful mother-of-pearl and diamond-encrusted hair barrette at the door. The two mermaids knocked and then dove to hide behind some nearby rocks. But only Jade's mom and dad came out. They picked up the barrette and, after a brief consultation, they began searching for the mermaids.

"Brynn, Priscilla," Mrs. Sands called as she checked all around her yard. "Don't be afraid, come here, we have something for you."

But Brynn and Priscilla had already swam away, headed for Will's house.

There, Priscilla left her designer handbag.

But only Will's brother was home.

They checked the local clamburger joint, the middle-school, and the speed-current stop, but no matter where they looked, there was no sign of Jade or Will.

"Where could they be?" Brynn asked.

"Let's think about this," said Priscilla. "What do we know? We know that both Jade and Will were wearing Swymbits."

"Right," said Brynn. "Which means their minds are being controlled by the sea witch."

"Right," said Priscilla. "And if the sea witch is trying to find us, which we know she is, then that means that Jade and Will are probably trying to find us, too."

"Priscilla, that's it!" said Brynn. "Of course! *They're* looking for *us*. And while I don't know where *you* would go, Will and Jade both know *my* favorite place to hide. I know exactly where to find them looking for me. Come on!"

Priscilla followed Brynn as she swam out of town. They swam carefully, darting from one hiding spot to the next.

"Where are we going?" asked Priscilla in a low voice.

"We're here," said Brynn.

They had come to the edges of the kelp forest.

CHAPTER TWENTY-TWO

The tall kelp waved back and forth in the tide. Shoals of silvery fish passed by, shifting and flashing in the sunlight. Sea stars moved slowly across the sea bottom. Hermit crabs and lobsters crawled here and there and sometimes darted into crags and crevices to escape predators. The sunlight shone magically through the blue-green water.

"Wowee," said Priscilla. "What a beautiful place!"

"I love it here," said Brynn. "I come here all the time with my pet sea turtle."

"You have a pet sea turtle?" said Priscilla. "That's amazing. You're so lucky! My parents won't let me have a pet—they're too afraid some precious artifact in the house might get knocked over and broken."

"Oh, Tully's the best," said Brynn. "If we ever get outta this mess, you'll have to come play with him."

"Brynn, thanks for being nice to me," said Priscilla suddenly.

"Who, me?" replied Brynn.

"Yeah. You might think I have lots of friends, but I don't. I miss my friends in Atlantis, and I haven't made many friends here. I'm glad we can get along, even though we didn't at first."

"Me, too," said Brynn.

They swam on through the long, lazily waving stalks of kelp. Soon they heard voices.

"Bryyynn? Brynn, where are you?"

Priscilla and Brynn turned to look at one another, their eyes open wide—it was Jade's voice.

"Brynn? Are you here? We wanna hang out with you!"

"That's Will!" said Brynn in an excited whisper.

Brynn and Priscilla shushed each other and stayed hidden.

"What should we do?" asked Priscilla.

"Do you know how to do a grab spell?" asked Brynn.

"I think so," said Priscilla. "That's the one Mrs. Meyers has been teaching us this week."

"Okay. We'll sneak around behind them and follow them for a while. When we're close enough, we'll snatch those Swymbits right off their wrists. I'll get Will's and you get Jade's."

"Sounds good," said Priscilla.

Both of them took a few moments to center themselves by closing their eyes and taking a few deep breaths. When they felt properly mindful, they drifted up out of their hiding place.

Brynn and Priscilla heard Will and Jade calling out again, and they swam in their direction. Soon they were following at a distance behind Will and Jade. They could see the green light flashing on the Swymbits. Priscilla and Brynn raised their hands, focused on the Swymbits, and wiggled their fingers with great dexterity.

Will and Jade didn't notice at first, but then the Swymbits began to shake and shift.

It's working! thought Brynn.

Then Will cried, "Hey!" and he slapped his hand over his Swymbit.

Jade did the same.

"Someone's using a grab spell to get our Swymbits," growled Will. He and Jade held tightly onto their Swymbits and looked around. Priscilla and Brynn tried to crouch in the cover of the kelp, but it was no use.

"It's Brynn!" shouted Will.

"And Priscilla!" yelled Jade.

"Let's get 'em!" cried Jade and Will together.

"Let's get outta here!" yelled Priscilla and Brynn together.

The mermaids took off through the forest, but Will and Jade were just a few tail wags behind them.

"Friendship amplifier!" cried Priscilla.

Brynn nodded frantically.

They clasped hands. The two hadn't had a chance to fight or say rude things to each other, and so their friendship was strong and clear. Their speed spell was instantly amplified, and they went rocketing through the water at an almost frightening speed.

After a few minutes of torpedoing through the kelp forest, Brynn and Priscilla stopped to rest, figuring that Will and Jade had been left in their wake. But they'd only stopped a moment when Jade and Will appeared again—they'd used a friendship amplifier, too.

Jade and Will lunged at Brynn and Priscilla, probably with the intent to wrap brand-new Swymbits around their wrists, but at the same time, Brynn and Priscilla were reaching for Jade's and Will's arms, trying to snatch their Swymbits off!

Round and round they swam and wrestled chaotically.

"This is like trying to herd catfish," mumbled Brynn.

"Sleep spell!" said Priscilla. She tried to whisper this into Brynn's ear, but the merkids were tumbling and somersaulting in the water like a pack of octopuses, and Will heard Priscilla's plan.

"Oh no you don't," said Will. He swam between them and scattered the mer-magic they had conjured.

Next Jade stopped and put her hands together, and Brynn knew she was casting a spell of some sort.

This is why I need to learn the bubble of protection spell! thought Brynn.

But just as Jade was growing her magical energy sphere, and concentrating on the spell, Priscilla swam up from behind and deftly unclasped her Swymbit. It spiraled down to the ocean floor.

Jade's expression changed first to one of surprise, then confusion, and then a sort of happy sleepiness, then back to confusion, and then to an expression that Brynn knew as just plain old Jade on a plain old day in the plain old ocean.

"What in the ocean is going on?" asked Jade. "Where am I?" She her head and turned looking way and that.

"No time to explain!" said Brynn.

She and Priscilla were closing in on Will.

"William Beach!" said Brynn. "You give me that silly Swymbit!"

Will, seeing he was outnumbered, turned tail and swam away as fast as he could.

"We can't let him get away!" said Brynn.

"I know what to do!" cried Priscilla. "Brynn! Sleep spell!"

"He's too far away!" groaned Brynn, motioning at Will, who now was nearly lost in the kelp.

"Just do it!" said Priscilla.

Brynn didn't know what Priscilla had in mind, but she knew whatever they did, they'd have to make it happen really quick—and Brynn trusted

Priscilla now, so she followed along and quickly started up a sleep spell.

"Jade!" cried Priscilla. "Our favorite song! One, two, and a one-two-three!"

Jade apparently also trusted Priscilla, because she sang right on Priscilla's cue, and the most amazing harmony filled the water.

So swim to me again! Just like you did last summer! Swim to me agaaaaain!

It was a gorgeous, thrilling sound, and it immediately pumped up Brynn's sleep spell to such a powerful level, Brynn wasn't sure she could even control it. But then it shot away toward Will and hit him in the tail like a charging killer whale. Will fell asleep instantly, drifting peacefully through the water like a merbaby at naptime.

Priscilla and Jade sang quietly now, like they were singing a lullaby to Will.

"Wowee!" said Brynn softly. "I love that song! You guys sound incredible. Your harmony is sending chills right to the end of my fins!"

The mermaids hurried over and laid Will down on a comfy rock. Will was snoring quietly, his hands tucked up under his cheek like a sea angel.

"Aw, he's so sweet-looking when he sleeps," observed Jade.

"Get that Swymbit off him!" said Priscilla, trying to keep her voice down so as not to wake Will.

Brynn unclasped the Swymbit. "Got it!"

The effect of breaking Phaedra's mind control must have broken the sleep spell too, and Will opened his eyes. On his face was first surprise, then confusion, then a happy dazed look, then confusion once more, and then finally the look they were all expecting—plain old Will.

"Whoa," said Will. He blinked and stretched and yawned. "Golly. I was having the most wonderful dream. I was at the JBATKW concert." He looked at Priscilla and then Jade and then Brynn. "And you were there. And you. And you!" He pointed at each one of them, then sat up. "Hey. What are you three doing in my bedroom?"

CHAPTER TWENTY-THREE

*B*rynn and Priscilla explained everything. They told Jade and Will all about the Swymbits and how the sea witch was using them to cast some kind of widespread control spell. They told them about how everyone had decided to fight against the humans and how Phaedra was going to teach the mers how to use magic to turn all the humans into sea slugs.

Jade made a face. "Gosh, all that happened?"

Brynn nodded. "And you were going to help!"

"I'm so glad you guys came around," said Jade. "I'd feel just awful if I'd turned hundreds of humans into sea slugs." She shuddered with revulsion.

"Me, too," said Will, and he shuddered, too.

And then Brynn and Priscilla told Will and Jade the plan they had developed. They drew diagrams in the sand and they pantomimed how the plan would unfold. When they'd finished, Will laughed.

"You know," he said, chuckling, "that's crazy enough that it just might work."

"What do you think, Jade?" asked Priscilla.

"It's fin-tastic!" said Jade. "I have some really smart friends. But I am worried about you being in danger, Brynn. The sea witch already tried to capture you once."

"That's why I'll have Will with me," said Brynn. "He's pulled my fins out of the fire more than once."

Will grinned.

Priscilla looked up toward the ocean surface. "The sun is setting. We better hurry."

"Let's do it," said Brynn.

That's when the mer-friends split up. Brynn and Will headed in one direction and Jade and Priscilla headed in another. All at once, Brynn realized that she felt completely comfortable about Priscilla working with Jade. She now understood that it was okay for friends to sometimes split up and spend time with other friends. It was okay to have different interests or to be working on different parts of a plan. Brynn had also discovered that Priscilla really was a fun, caring mermaid, just as Jade and Will had said.

I guess now I have three *best friends*, thought Brynn, and although she was afraid, Brynn smiled as she swam along with Will.

Although she was feeling better about her friendship situation, Brynn was feeling quite nervous about their plan with the sea witch. It was one thing to make a plan and talk about carrying it out, it was quite another thing to swim directly toward danger. And now that Brynn had accidentally come up with the idea of turning people into sea slugs, she worried that the sea witch really might do that to her after all.

And there was always the chance of something unexpected happening.

"Brynn I'm going to put my bubble of protection on you now," said Will as they swam toward the Craggy Deep, where Phaedra had planned to meet her followers.

Brynn bit the inside of her cheek. It was so frustrating to not be able to do that basic spell for herself. Would she ever learn?

"But Will, won't you need it?"

"You're the one we're using as the bait," said Will. "I'm more worried about you."

Brynn nodded, though she didn't particularly like being called "the bait." While they swam, Brynn tried to calm herself by taking deep breaths and thinking of her favorite places and people, like the kelp forest and her pet sea turtle and her friends.

When they reached the edge of the cavernous Craggy Deep, Will and Brynn didn't have to search around very much to find Phaedra and the mob of seafolk who followed her. They saw the huge crowd right away. It looked as though the entire town of

Fulgent was gathered there, along with many dagons and selkies.

"Look, there's your mom," Brynn whispered to Will as she pointed.

"And there's your parents," said Will.

Sure enough, there in the crowd of mers were Dana and Adrian, listening carefully and even nodding in agreement as the sea witch spoke.

"The great merfolk of Fulgent have a long history as protectors of the ocean and guardians of the sea," Phaedra cried. Her voice was amplified with magic. It sounded forceful and yet lovely, loud and yet musical. She was a very great public speaker. "You have helped the whales and dolphins and sharks. You have protected the shellfish and crustaceans and mollusks. You've been a friend to the most massive and the tiniest creatures in the sea."

The giant crowd shouted their approval.

Phaedra continued. "Now it is time to deal with the true enemy of our way of life and all life beneath the ocean. The humans!"

The crowd shouted some more. Will's mom, Brynn's parents, and all the dagons and selkies and the once-peaceful merfolk of Fulgent were hollering in angry agreement with Phaedra.

"The humans pollute our waters, litter our shores, and destroy the beautiful seascapes where we live!"

More shouting.

"It ends tonight!" cried Phaedra, stabbing her

upward into the dark, swirling waters. "Tonight we swim through the ocean to remove and destroy any human presence. Tonight we take back the ocean. Are you with me?"

The crowd erupted in applause and hoots and hollering. Merfolk waved their arms and tails to show their agreement. And with so many from Fulgent in one place, it was easy to see all the Swymbits blinking steadily with that eerie green light.

"Are you ready?" Will asked.

"I guess," said Brynn. "But there's so many of them now. I didn't expect the entire town to show up. I'm not sure if this will work or not."

"So," Will said, "Are you ready?

"I guess I have to be," said Brynn, pressing her lips together. She poked the giant bubble of protection that Will had used his magic to create. She was relieved to find that the bubble was quite strong.

"Just remember, I'll be right here," said Will. "I can see everything from here, and I'll be amplifying your speed spell with our friendship."

Phaedra went on lecturing to the gathered merfolk. Her voice reverberated into the massive trench of the Craggy Deep and echoed back ominously. She raised her hands and gestured grandly as she spoke. When she paused, the mers responded loudly with applause and more wild shouts.

"And now, my honored and beloved merfolk of

Fulgent—who is ready to learn how to magically solve all our problems? Who is ready to learn the magic to turn these lowly humans into lowly sea slugs?"

Now the crowd rose up higher in the water with arms uplifted, and shouted and clapped even more thunderously.

Brynn frowned. "That won't solve all our problems."

"You better go," said Will. "If our plan doesn't work—"

"It'll work," said Brynn. "It has to."

These were brave words, but as Brynn darted away through the water, she felt unsure. She had a sickening feeling in her stomach that she might end the day with a new life—that of a sea slug.

CHAPTER TWENTY-FOUR

*B*ravery is doing what you know to be right, even though you may have to face your fears or dangers. That is why it is possible to be very courageous and yet trembling in fear all over. And that is what Brynn was doing: she was so nervous about being caught by the sea witch and being used as an example for her sea slug spell that she was quaking from head to tail. She tried to calm herself. She tried being mindful and centered.

She thought of the people she loved and those who loved her. She thought of people she knew who were brave. There was her mom, Dana, who was brave enough to find new friends when she was bullied in school. Her father, Adrian, went on countless and sometimes dangerous missions to do his part as a sea guardian. There was Priscilla, who'd moved to a new town where she didn't know anyone. And Brynn could not forget Jade and Will, who had helped protect humans and stopped the sea witch, even at risk of being hurt. Mrs. Sands—Jade's mom—regularly faced difficult challenges that scared her in her work as a doctor. And then there were all the merfolk who routinely responded to the dolphin calls when help was needed in the ocean.

Did they refuse to help when there was an oil spill and black sludge had coated all the marine life nearby? No. Hundreds of mers responded to the call —caring and cleaning the animals and beaches and coral.

Did they stay home during a violent storm when a family had been involved in an accident on the speed-current? No. They'd gone, even as the wind and water whipped them about. Adrian had helped at that one.

Brynn could think of countless news stories she had seen or heard about in which a merperson displayed remarkable bravery even in the face of danger or fear or difficulty. The merfolk believed in the mer-oath: *We are protectors of the ocean, guardians of the sea. Wherever living things need help, that's where we'll be.*

The mers would take all steps possible to be safe, of course, but risk of danger did not stop them from helping, and it was all because they believed in the mer-oath.

And Brynn believed in it, too.

Even though her heart pounded and her hands shook and her throat felt tight, she knew it wasn't right to hurt others.

Come on, Brynn, she told herself, *do this for the humans.* And she kept telling herself that as she swam right up to the back of the crowd. She swam up behind them, but not too close, and then she swam a little higher, until she was floating above them, so that they could hear her clearly. Then she waited for a lull in the cheering and lecturing, and with all her strength she bellowed, "HEY!"

Phaedra had opened her mouth to make another loud proclamation, but she stopped when Brynn shouted. Then Phaedra blinked a few times and looked around, trying to see where the interruption had come from. When she saw Brynn, her face took on a furious expression.

And in another moment, every mermaid and merman and dagon and selkie turned to look at Brynn, too. With hundreds of eyes on her, Brynn suddenly felt very small, helpless, and not at all brave, and she knew she had made a tremendous mistake.

"It isn't right to hurt others," she said in a voice that wasn't quite as loud as she'd intended. Her voice also quavered a little, too, and she thought she might begin to cry. But she took a deep breath and continued. "Stop what you're doing! It's not okay!"

For a moment, the crowd was silent. No one said

a word, not even Phaedra. Perhaps they were awaiting instructions from Phaedra herself. Or, maybe they were all so entirely shocked by Brynn that no one knew what to do.

But then the edges of Phaedra's lips curl into a smile.

"Get her," hissed Phaedra. "Bring her to me."

The crowd followed Phaedra's command and moved all at once as though they themselves were a huge wave of water, moving as one giant beast. They quickly began to envelop her like an enormous octopus. They swam out to Brynn's left and right. They swam above and below her. Their Swymbits flashed steadily.

"Oh, no," cried Brynn as they surged forward. She caught sight of her parents in the crowd. "Mom? Dad?"

But her pleas made no difference. They went along with the crowd in a joint mission to capture Brynn and bring her to Phaedra.

"Well," Brynn said suddenly to the massive crowd, "That's all I had to tell you. Gotta go!"

She turned on her tail and dashed away. A few in the crowd dove forward very quickly, and several more were already conjuring their own speed spells. However, Brynn had a healthy head-start, and she was already swimming with her own speed spell, which was being amplified by Will from his hiding place.

A middle schooler with a speed spell could move pretty fast, but there were full-grown mermaids and mermen who could swim almost as fast with no speed spells. Selkies were particularly quick in the water. And there were many in Fulgent who were known for their speed. How long could Brynn outrun them with her head-start and amplified speed spell? She didn't know, but she knew where she was going, and she was going to try her hardest.

Brynn chanced a look behind her and saw that several merfolk and selkies were already just a few tail wags behind her. They clawed and kicked furiously through the water, grabbing and reaching for her tail. Brynn swam harder.

"Bring her to meee!" howled the sea witch from behind the swarm of seafolk.

Brynn had a sudden picture in her mind as herself as a sea slug, and this made her swim a little faster. Or maybe it was Will's friendship amplification. There was no telling which it was, but little Brynn suddenly zipped ahead again, leaving those in pursuit to wonder how she was swimming so fast.

But Brynn was quickly tiring out. She was breathing hard and her tail muscles ached from effort. She was almost at her destination, but now she wondered if she could make it that far.

So tired, she thought. *So, so, so tired.*

And then, there it was in the distance—the dark mouth of a huge cave. The sight of it was blurry in

Brynn's eyes as she swam frantically, and she didn't know how far she had still to go, but she was getting closer! The cave mouth grew larger as she swam onward, but the mob of seafolk behind her was upon her. She kicked harder. Several strong hands grabbed at Brynn, but the protection bubble that Will had cast did its job, and she kept swimming.

I'm almost there!

Then a magical energy sphere struck Brynn from behind, and Will's protection bubble popped, leaving only a shower of purple and pink sparks all around Brynn. She spiraled and tumbled forward, completely out of control.

Almost there!

Someone grabbed Brynn by her tail. Then someone had her arms. Soon the crowd of Phaedra followers completely swallowed Brynn. She was captured, but through the swarm of grabbing hands, angry faces, and green blinking lights, Brynn saw the smooth walls and cavernous inside of Mammoth Cave.

CHAPTER TWENTY-FIVE

*B*rynn was sure these were her last moments as a mermaid. The rest of her days would be spent as a lowly sea slug. She was very sad about this. She really liked being a mermaid. She loved combing her long lavender mermaid hair and polishing her beautiful mermaid tail scales. She loved doing mer-magic and swimming through the ocean.

She couldn't believe this was probably going to be her last moments as a mermaid.

What would it be like as a sea slug? What did sea slugs even do? She knew from her studies at school that sea slugs were "gastropods," which meant they were mostly just one big stomach. And although some sea slugs were colorful and maybe even what you might call beautiful, they were just small and squishy blobs that drifted or crawled through the sea eating "detritus," which was basically sea dust and litter and rubbish.

This didn't sound like very much fun to Brynn.

But she was only half-awake now, exhausted from swimming so hard and being zapped out of Will's protection bubble. She only knew that she was now being held fast by dozens or maybe even hundreds of seafolk.

"Hold her steady!" said a loud and lovely voice.

It was Phaedra, of course.

Brynn blinked and squinted through the forest of seafolk and saw Phaedra coming closer. A few of the merfolk and selkies and dagons moved aside and made way. Phaedra came forward, her terrible beauty lighting up the water around her.

"Move aside. I will do this myself this time, rather than trusting one of you dunces to do it for me." In her long beautiful hand, Phaedra held a Swymbit.

Brynn thought, *so she isn't going to turn me into a sea slug after all. That's nice, I guess.*

Phaedra wrapped the Swymbit around Brynn's wrist and buckled it on tightly. Brynn's thoughts swam sickeningly for a few moments, and then something odd happened. Instead of fearing Phaedra, she began to be rather fond of her. Brynn suddenly felt that Phaedra was good, reasonable, and helpful. Brynn never thought of this before, but she realized then that she really wanted to cooperate with Phaedra.

Brynn smiled a weird, sleepy smile and said "Oh. Hello, Phaedra. You look very pretty today."

Phaedra smiled back at Brynn, but it was a devious, unkind smile.

Somewhere down in Brynn's mind, she knew something bad was happening. She was having the same thoughts that everyone else in Fulgent had been having—thoughts of sinking ships and hurting humans and using anger and violence to solve problems. But the reasonable part of Brynn's mind, the part that made her want to be kind and helpful, was pushed down and told to be quiet.

At last, Brynn had come under the control of the sea witch.

Then, through the fog of Phaedra's anger and control and her wicked magic, Brynn heard a noise. It was just a humming at first, but then it grew louder and more beautiful. It was a musical note. Someone was singing. A mermaid somewhere was singing a high, clear note.

Then another voice joined in, and the two voices were harmonizing in the most dazzling way Brynn could remember. Then a song began, the harmony pure and sweet. Even with the Phaedra fog on her mind, Brynn saw that all the seafolk in the cave froze completely. And they looked around frantically, trying to identify and locate the sound.

The singing seemed not to come from one direction or another, but from all around them, because this was Mammoth Cave, with its strange and lovely acoustics. Brynn looked around, too, and there on the stage, just where their voices could carry best, were Priscilla and Jade. The two talented mermaids had been practicing singing their song together every day for weeks, and their singing ability exceeded anything heard in Fulgent in many years. This singing was so beautiful, in fact, that it became magic.

In the huge expanse of Mammoth Cave, the music became threads of glittering gold mer-magic, which snaked gracefully through the water and all around and between the seafolk. They looked here and there, distracted and confused and charmed.

Later on, Brynn would also remember seeing William Beach swimming quietly through Mammoth Cave. He swam in a sneaky way, as though he did not want to be noticed by the sea witch or anyone else in the cave. And no one did notice him. He quietly but quickly swam up behind Brynn, slipped the Swymbit off her wrist, and led her blinking and bewildered to the Mammoth Cave stage.

The singing continued, growing louder and even more beautiful. Some of the seafolk seemed pleased by the music. Others seemed to fear the golden threads of musical magic. Even Phaedra seemed impressed, but puzzled, too. For a moment all she could do was listen and look with a dumbfounded expression.

Then she shook her head, raised herself up in the water, and said, "Ignore that dreadful caterwauling and pay attention to me, you mindless fish!"

The seafolk in the crowd shook their heads, too. Some poked fingers into their ears.

But then the music stopped suddenly.

"Now," said Priscilla.

On that signal, Priscilla, Jade, Will, and Brynn sang out loud and clear:

Awwww-eee, awww-oooooo. Rest your eyes, close them now, and sleep. Sleep so deep. Go to sleep. Awwww-eeeeeee, Awwwwww-oooooo.

Jade and Priscilla's voices harmonized perfectly, and Will's voice joined in a lower register. Brynn sang along, too, but mostly she was filled with relief and happiness at hearing the sweet melody. The effect was a musical burst of magic that fell over the selkies and merpeople and dagons, and in an instant they fell asleep. Brynn and her friends had wondered if the magical spell would work on Phaedra, but they couldn't see her now.

"Wowee," whispered Brynn.

The friends swam out among the slumbering seafolk. All around them was the sound of snoring and deep breathing.

The friends laughed, but quietly.

"It worked!" whispered Brynn. "I thought I was going to be a sea slug, for sure!"

"We're not quite done yet," Will pointed out.

"You've got to finish this, Brynn. The sleep spell won't last long."

Brynn nodded. "Okay. Give me some room."

She took a few breaths, and then one last deep breath, before belting out the loudest, highest pitched note she could.

"Aaarrrhhh!" Brynn sang. "La la laaahh!

This was not beautiful music. It was indeed cater-wauling, and it bounced and boomed off the smooth walls of Mammoth Cave like a hundred walruses tumbling down a staircase.

At this, all seafolk woke up and most of them covered their ears, but in the same moment, all of their Swymbits not only stopped working, but cracked open, popping and fizzling in tiny green fountains of angry sea-lectronic sparks.

CHAPTER TWENTY-SIX

Brynn quickly found her parents among all the other seafolk. They were sitting on the edge of the stage blinking and shaking their heads and looking around. Everyone else in Mammoth Cave seemed to be doing the same thing.

"Where am I?" they murmured.

"What's going on?" they groaned.

"What's everyone doing here?" they mumbled.

With all the Swymbits shorted-out and shattered, the trance over the merfolk, selkies, and dagons was likewise broken.

"Mom? Dad?" cried Brynn. "Are you all right?"

"What am I doing here?" said Adrian.

"Yeah, and where's here?" asked Dana. "Isn't this Mammoth Cave?"

"It's a long story," said Brynn. "But before I tell

you, I've got to tell the police and we've got to find Phaedra."

Soon Brynn and her friends had found practically the entire Fulgent police force. After explaining the situation, the Fulgent police officers searched the cave for Phaedra. She was quickly located. She was hiding in one of the alcoves in the back of Mammoth Cave, furiously tapping at her destroyed Swymbit, but every time she did, red sparks shot out.

"Why won't this lousy thing work?" muttered Phaedra. "Such shoddy workmanship!" At first, she didn't notice the search party and went on tapping at the fritzing Swymbit.

Officer McScales stepped forward and sternly said, "Phaedra, you're under arrest!"

Her head snapped up from the Swymbit, and she glared fiercely at McScales and the others.

"Oh piffle, you clam brain!" snapped Phaedra. "Me? Under arrest! You're under my control, you worm!"

"Not anymore, ma'am," said Officer McScales. "Looks like you've failed again. Now come with us, please."

"I'm free!" cried Phaedra. "You were all there at the courthouse. I am not guilty! Now go away until I get this silly Swymbit working again. Go! Shoo!"

"Ma'am," said McScales firmly, "it's illegal under mer-law to cast control spells on people. Especially entire towns. We're taking you into custody."

He and several other mer-police swam forward.

Phaedra hurled her malfunctioning Swymbit to the rocky ground, where it splintered into a final little burst of magical red sparks. Then Phaedra's eyes darted from face to face. She looked like a cornered rat-fish. Her gaze at last fell on Brynn, Jade, Will, and Priscilla.

"So, it's just as I suspected," sneered Phaedra. "It was you and your friends, eh, Ms. Finley? You and your nosy, meddling, little friends!"

Brynn shrugged sheepishly and nodded.

"Well, I'm afraid you'll never take me this time!" hissed Phaedra, and just as McScales and other mer-police were about to seize her, Phaedra slipped into a crevice in the wall behind her, vanishing into the shadows.

Brynn and the others later found out that there was a secret network of tunnels in the alcoves of Mammoth Cave. No one had explored them in years, but Phaedra was a collector of secrets, and she'd made her escape. The mer-police searched for days afterwards, but never found a trace of the sea witch.

Brynn and her friends and family helped the rest of the Fulgent Swymbit wearers figure out where they were, where they'd been, and where to go next. There was lots of confusion and disorientation.

Judge Matthew Waterly, one of the smartest citizens of Fulgent, tried to help everyone understand.

"I'm afraid we've been the victims of a horrible

control spell," said the judge. "It was cast through our consumer sea-lectronics, into our brains, and the culprit was Phaedra the sea witch!"

There was murmuring in the crowd and the seafolk began taking off their ruined Swymbits.

"Furthermore," said the judge, "it seems she may have tampered with some of our views and opinions. For example, she apparently made us so hostile to the humans, she was getting ready to have us turn them all into sea slugs! Fortunately, those effects should have all worn off, now that the Swymbits have been destroyed."

"Not for me!" said one merman with long black beard.

"Yeah, I still feel that way!" said a nearby selkie.

"This doesn't change the fact that the humans killed part of the coral reef," shouted a dagon. "They pollute the sea and make life miserable for us! They deserve to be stopped. And punished!"

"No," said Brynn. "That doesn't mean we should hurt them."

"They need to be stopped," cried Ian Fletcher, holding up a fist.

"I agree," said a mermaid who Brynn recognized as a math teacher from school. "The humans must stop their toxic ways, but we must *teach* them, not *harm* them."

Others in the crowd responded. "Yes, kindness and cooperation is the merfolk way!"

Soon the entire cave was in a minor uproar, as various groups debated about their opinions.

Brynn turned to her parents. "I don't understand. Why are they still siding with the sea witch even though they don't have the Swymbits anymore?"

"Not everyone agrees with the sea witch," said Dana. "And not everyone agrees with each other. But look, Brynn," Dana pointed at the various seafolk. "They have different opinions, but they're not angry or violent now. In fact, most of them are being polite. We don't all have to agree.

"Yeah," said Adrian, "and with the sea witch out of our hair for a while, we're hopefully free to settle our differences civilly and according to the law."

Brynn shrugged. She was bothered that not everyone agreed, but she didn't always agree with her friends or parents. She thought about it for a few moments and then said, "I guess the only way we'll agree on everything is if we bring Phaedra back to control our minds, huh?"

"Now you've got it," Dana said with a smile.

Her parents seemed less disoriented now, and so they all began swimming to the mouth of Mammoth Cave to go home. Will and Jade and Priscilla had collected their parents and followed along.

"I have something that I want to share," said Brynn.

"Well, let's hear it," said Adrian.

"Yeah, what is it?" asked Will.

"I don't know what should be done about the humans and their pollution," she said, "but I've only got a few days to pick out an outfit for the Jay Barracuda and the Killer Whales show!"

CHAPTER TWENTY-SEVEN

*N*ow that people knew the Swymbits had been used by Phaedra to control them, no one wanted to buy them anymore.

"What will your parents do now?" Brynn had asked Priscilla at lunch the next day.

Priscilla shrugged. "Father and Mother will find something else to sell. They're always saying that good business is about being adaptable."

Brynn was just glad the Priscilla's family had decided to stay—despite the Swymbit disaster. A lot had changed in the last few weeks. Brynn no longer viewed Priscilla as a threat or an enemy. She realized that Priscilla was just another mermaid, like she was. Maybe some things were easier for Priscilla, Brynn sure wouldn't mind an Orpheus Shell or getting to model for *Young Mermaid*, but there were things she had that Priscilla didn't—like a really awesome sea turtle and Adrian and Dana for parents. Brynn had made the decision that instead of comparing herself to Priscilla, she'd instead look for the things they had in common. When she did that, it was easy to make Priscilla her friend.

In fact, it was Priscilla who had come up with the idea to form a club at school to help clean up the ocean. It was just what Brynn hoped for to help save the coral reef. While she knew they wouldn't be able to clean everything, they could at least make a difference and that was a start.

The afternoon of their first meeting, Priscilla gave everyone who came bright colored t-shirts that read, "Clean Team," and Priscilla worked just as hard, or harder, than anyone else. She didn't mind breaking a nail or getting her scales dirty to help save the coral, and Brynn admired her for it. Jade and Priscilla had singing in common, but Brynn and Priscilla both had a passion for helping others and saving the coral reef.

The morning of the Jay Barracuda concert, Brynn got a phone call.

"Brynn!" squealed Jade over the shell-phone. "You aren't going to believe this! Priscilla can get us front row VIP tickets to the concert, including back-stage passes!"

"Oh, wow," said Brynn. "That's really cool!"

"I know, right," said Jade. "It's fin-tastic! So, we'll come by in the sea-copter to pick you up in about an hour."

"Actually," said Brynn. "I already have plans to go to the concert with my dad."

"Really?" said Jade. "Well, I'm sure if you explained, he'd let you come with us instead."

"No, I want to go with my dad, but if you have a spare ticket, I know someone else who would really love to go," said Brynn.

The mermaids finished their call, and then Brynn hung up. But when she turned around, she found her dad behind her with a funny smile on his face and his arms folded.

"Brynn," he said. "It's okay. You can go with your friends. I don't mind."

"No, I really do want to go with you," said Brynn. "It was the only thing that could cheer me up a while ago. It'll be fun!"

"I'm not sure our seats in the nosebleed section will be quite as fun as VIP tickets," said Adrian.

"It's not about where you are at the concert, it's just about getting to go! It'll be tons of fun," said Brynn. "Besides, just knowing that they're going to give the extra ticket to Will is enough. He's going to lose his mind when they tell him!"

At the concert that night, Brynn and Adrian sang and danced and laughed as Jay Barracuda and the Killer Whales performed. Brynn knew more of the words than her dad, but he caught on fast. Brynn was completely astounded by the lights and the costumes and everything else. And when Jay Barracuda sang,

Brynn really felt like he was singing just to her. She held her hands to her chest and sighed.

"Are you sure you wouldn't rather be up-front with your friends?" shouted Adrian over the thumping drums and wailing guitars.

"Oh, no," said Brynn. "I'm happy right here. In fact, I'm the luckiest mermaid in the world!" The father and daughter spun in circles, making a wave of bubbles. Brynn peered down at the seats in the front row of the stage and saw her friends Will, Priscilla, and Jade. They were having the time of their lives, dancing, grooving, and singing along. Brynn was happy they were all there, together (kind of), and she knew they'd be talking about this for weeks, but she wouldn't trade her nosebleed seats with her dad for all the VIP seats in the sea.

PLEASE LEAVE A REVIEW

Please take a moment to review A Mermaid In Middle Grade on Amazon as this helps other readers to find the story. Thank you!

In print and ebooks

Hannah Saves the World (releasing fall/winter 2020)

A Mermaid in Middle Grade

Book 4: The Deep Sea Scroll (releasing fall/winter 2020)

Book 5: The Golden Trident (releasing winter 2020)

Book 6: The Great Old One (releasing 2021)

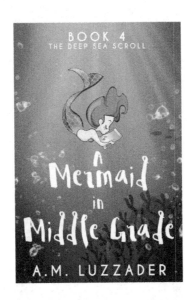

BOOK 4
THE DEEP SEA SCROLL

A
Mermaid
in
Middle Grade

A.M. LUZZADER

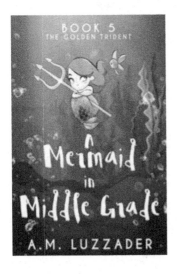

BOOK 5
THE GOLDEN TRIDENT

A
Mermaid
in
Middle Grade

A.M. LUZZADER

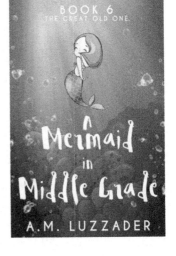

BOOK 6
THE GREAT OLD ONE

A
Mermaid
in
Middle Grade

A.M. LUZZADER

ABOUT THE AUTHOR

A.M. Luzzader writes middle-grade books for children and science fiction books for adults. She is a self-described 'fraidy cat. Things she will run away from include (but are not limited to): mice, snakes, spiders, bits of string and litter that resemble spiders, most members of the insect kingdom, and (most especially) bats. Bats are the worst. But A.M. is first and primarily a mother to two energetic and intelligent sons, and this role inspires and informs her writing.

A.M.'s favorite things include cats, strawberries, and summer. She was named Writer of the Year for 2019 by the League of Utah Writers. A.M. invites readers to visit her website at www.amandaluzzader.com and her Facebook page www.facebook.com/authoramandaluzzader.

Visit www.subscribepage.com/amandaluzzader to sign up to receive an occasional newsletter with information about promotions and new releases. From this site you'll also be able to download a **Free Activity Kit for A Mermaid in Middle Grade.**

Made in the USA
Monee, IL
12 December 2020

52599760R00134